THE TRIAL

OF

SALLINIQUAI

A prequel to
The Salliniquai Chronicles

STELLA FLETTON

THE TRIAL OF SALLINIQUAI

Text Copyright © 2022 Stella Fletton

Cover photo-illustration © 2023 Stella Fletton

REVIEWS

Join Juggernaut, Smudge-face, and Sally as they try to work out what exactly happened THAT weekend, and what the hell is an orballoon anyway?!

Stella effortlessly draws you into the world of the Empress, who is so ready to draw in the Aquarian age, yet still clueless on the reality of the Earthly realm.

What adventures will follow her impetuousness as she learns four deeply spiritual lessons in the mortal realm? Read on and find out!

Stella's first novel is a fast-paced, mystery that leaves you wanting more. Her attention to detail means you can listen to the music, and pick up any book mentioned for yourself, allowing you to expand your own knowledge and wisdom.

The delightful way in which she weaves in Pagan themes, and her favourite places gives the book a spiritual and other-worldly feel yet leaves you feeling you could join the girls for their pizza party, you just have to knock on the door!

A must read for 2024!

Charlotte Pardy MA
Pagan Priestess and Psychotherapist

"A fantastic and spellbinding story ... "

Philip Carr-Gomm
Author of *Druid Mysteries*

Marvellacious! *The Salliniquai Chronicles has unique fantasy realms with fresh concepts and extraordinary characters unlike any others. If the seeker's quest in THE CELESTINE PROPHECY (James Redfield) resonates, and if you enjoyed the multicultural dynamics of WHITE TEETH (Zadie Smith) and like the subtle, spiritually atmospheric feel of DUNE, the 2021 remake (adapted from the 1965 novel by Frank Herbert.) Then, you will love THE SALLINIQUAI CHRONICLES.*

A. T. Flowers
Author of *The Serenity Experience*

DEDICATION

For Rachel Doris Bernard
My strength, my spirituality, my Mum.

ACKNOWLEDGEMENTS

A huge thank you to the readers whose comments and feedback inspired me to keep going. Ben Fletton, Anna James, Kristin Hammel, Kate Oram, Kandyce Walters, Sue Trudgian, and Joanne Walter.

CONTENTS

The Trial of Salliniquai

A NOTE FROM THE TIMEKEEPER

The **T references** that appear in all books in THE SALLINIQUAI CHRONICLES series refer to sections of Salliniquai's story that provide a secondary level of detail with regards to characters, scenery, conversations, shenanigans, revelations, official procedures, and such. These excerpts can be found in *The Books of Malsimily Translations. (Vols 1 and 2)*

Prologue

In the human physical realm. Earth.

Rowanshire, England. Friday 28th February, 2020.

Sally Vincent-Payne's unusually distinctive, sea-green eyes were slightly glazed as she stood alone in her bedroom looking out the part-frosted window at nothing in particular. The estate she lived on was a landscape of identical snow-covered houses with newly fallen snow turning to grey slush on the ground and frost in the trees dripping sparkling water drops from the leaves. While students, parents with young children, dog walkers and such made their way through the estate passing her house as they did so, she was day dreaming about Saint Lucia while waiting for her cat, Serenity, to appear at the window.

She jumped a little as her phone vibrated in her blazer pocket and she quickly dug it out. At the picture ID of her friend's grinning face, she smiled indulgently at the phone's screen and touched it to open the message. It read:

"Today is my birthday!!!" As if she needed reminding. "Ready for a rad weekend, Bubbs?"

"Totally ready, Smudge :-)" She sent back, as excited as her friend by their plans. "See you in ten." She added, glancing around the room to confirm she had not forgotten anything. Picking up her two bags, one for school and one for her overnight stay, she started towards the door. She paused halfway across the room, having noticed her unique little book, The Serenity Experience, standing upright on her side table. She stared at it for a moment. The position it was in was not the way she had left it, and the cover was behaving oddly again, doing its weird, smoky, swirling thing ...

From somewhere beyond the human physical realm, a mystical being of great power chose that moment to subtly manipulate time. Infused with magic, the air began to thicken and swirl around her, and suddenly, everything stopped. Mesmerised for exactly nine minutes, Sally, unable to tear her gaze away from the book, was frozen in place.

In the magical Realm of the Empress, during those nine minutes ...

In a giant amethyst geode, the Elevated One, an imposing, androgynous being with a dark brown face partly hidden beneath a veil, stood on a dais with their rune-infused staff gripped firmly in one hand. The power they commanded snapped and crackled at their fingertips and flashed like silver lightning in their eyes as they focussed on weaving a spell. Their actions created a close, musty aroma that permeated the air, and began to build in intensity.

Hovering beside them, the androgynous Timekeeper, a manipulator of time and the translator of all events relating to the life and quest of the Empress, worked their numerous time translation rings.

Time translation rings were an impossible, yet actual, mix of several solid and fluid substances that spun at different heights and speeds in either direction. They could enlarge, project images, and blend into and out of the unseen. Worn on all four fingers of both hands, the rings were operated with incredible speed, making the Timekeeper's swiftly moving fingers mind-bogglingly creepy to watch.

Blessed with the gift of foresight, and having considered what was coming, the Timekeeper helped to create three essential situations and conditions to impact the Empress's lives in the human physical realm. Before coming to the Elevated One's geode, they had been with the Alchemist in the cradle, creating the first two. A thriving new county in England called Rowanshire and an area in Saint Lucia called The Lavender Valley. Working with the Elevated One, their combined magical powers would create the third. An important book called Spiritual Illumination. Three fictitious things which, in due course, would become realities.

The two were searching for a human host for Empress Salliniquai. A young girl from Rowanshire with a unique type of energy, and ties to the island of Saint Lucia, because this was the location of the jump portal back to the Realm of the Empress. Soon enough, one appeared, and as the Timekeeper worked their rings slightly differently, a distinct, silvery glow brightened their eyes. The exact moment to manipulate the human girl had arrived.

"The time translation has started, and the flashback links are forming now. Infusion shall begin on the evening before it all kicks off ... right ... about ... there, while she sleeps," The Timekeeper said, manoeuvring their fingers over a heavy ring of a metallic, burgundy hue. It doubled in size, projecting a clear picture of a football-sized orb, in a silvery-purple shade, before them. As the image slowly faded, it revealed the face of a young girl with honey-coloured skin and a gap-toothed smile.

The time aspect of the Timekeeper's rings slowed momentarily as the translation element initiated. The projection ceased, and the ring abruptly returned to its standard size. The Timekeeper drew back a little and their robe, which had appeared solid while they hovered in place, became layered in smoky shadows as they moved, giving them an ethereal presence.

Ignoring the strange, *kicks off* reference, the Elevated One asked, "What object did you choose to infuse the Kee? The collar or the orb?"

"We chose the orb."

"Once the process begins, how long before the infusion is complete?"

"Around nine hours."

The Elevated One considered a moment. "From the morning, then?"

"It is as you say."

Satisfied with their response, the Elevated One nodded as they considered the construction of the spell they would have to complete when the future situation arose. A lock of their golden-black hair had fallen outside the finely woven hood of their slick, leathery robe, and they casually brushed it back behind their ear. The scent of Raynorlorium wafted around them now, arising from their spell casting.

"So, if she does this, although we cannot reverse it, we can be certain of her return." It was a statement rather than a question.

The Timekeeper's closely cropped, purple-black hair accentuated their edgy, ebony-black face as they turned towards the Elevated One slightly and nodded, their fingers working.

"*When* she does this," they corrected. "We have seen to it by way of the clown and the brothers." The Timekeeper and The Elevated One exchanged a few more words before the Elevated One nodded again, indicating their acceptance of the Timekeeper's actions.

"For the love of the Empress."

"For the love of the Empress." The Timekeeper responded, preparing to depart. Their hands lowered, but two of their fingers continued to work. The Elevated One had to act accordingly during a later event, so shrouding this meeting in a hold-time spell had been essential to take the memory of the exchange from them. It was a necessary step very much within their authority to take. The Timekeeper's magic left no trace unless they wanted it to, and on this occasion, the Elevated One was none the wiser as they watched them go, a hint of mild curiosity in their eyes.

Due to time functioning differently in the Realm of the Empress, the observation and initiation process took exactly nine seconds to complete.

In the human physical realm...

When time returned to normal, and Sally's awareness returned to the present, she was holding the book standing in front of her side table. Blinking thrice quickly, she glanced at the clock and frowned, her head slightly cocked to one side. Time had run away from her somehow. She would be late meeting Smudge-face and the Juggernaut in Ashington Park if she did not hurry. She paused to sniff the air, wondering briefly where the strong, sharp smell of

Raynorlorium's (lemons to your earthly folk) had come from. After a final sweeping glance around the room, she rushed out the door.

In the magical Realm of the Empress...

At a time outside of the linear, the brilliant, emerald green orb transporting the Empress Salliniquai, First Daughter of House Triumphant to the Geodes of the Elevated One, glided through a sky of an unheard of silvery-green hue with purpose. Moving towards a magnificent sun that never set but turned within an enormous, gloriously bright symbol of Venus, she passed over her self-created fields. Giant, smoky Rain bows rose and thumped down into the ground. Trees with massive, mattress-sized leaves reached towards the sky, and a vast, upright ocean, with no visible barrier holding it back, stood as a gateway to the Distance realm and the realms beyond.

Salliniquai looked down at the field of ice diamonds, their jagged, uneven points jutting out from a sea of ice. The field of purple night blooms, swaying in the breeze and at other sights of pure wonder. Her Empresserial chime and the sound of the never-ending wind were constants within the realm, along with powerful, deep-rooted magic, the signs of which were everywhere and normal.

The orb arrived at the sight of the three geodes, floated towards the large amethyst, and lowered to the ground. Its brightness dimmed, and after stepping out, Salliniquai glanced around to see if the Elevated One was present. No sign. Good. Although she had arrived a whole sun turn early for her next lesson, just as she had planned, she stayed alert and watchful for the slightest sign of their return.

Dressed in a robe of an indeterminate, softly floating substance more liquid than material, Salliniquai was a striking figure with a naturally regal posture and composure. She was of royal lineage with an entitled manner, and the ever-present soft glow around her indicated the presence of an immeasurable, powerful magic continually kept in check by her will alone.

Having grown frustrated with always doing what her guardians said *without question* because it was for the good of the whole, right now, she did not feel an ounce of guilt for her actions. Sending her orb into the unseen with a mere thought, she approached the Elevated One's inky-black karm, Shi-linga, sitting on her haunches just within the entry. It would not do for it to alert the Elevated One to her presence. She reached up to gently stroke the side of her head and willed her to rest. The huge karm began to purr, and then it settled its head onto its paws, lay down and closed its eyes.

Hurriedly crossing the empty, hollow interior of the geode towards the raised dais built into the curving, crystalised wall at the rear, she climbed the centrally located steps, then angled left towards the circle of travelling earth. With a smug, satisfied sigh, she stood gazing down upon the open flower portal nestled within. In her last lesson with the Elevated One, she had nodded understandingly in all the right places as they instructed her, keeping her expression neutral but interested as she secretly planned her escape.

Of course, she remembered her obligation to prepare for the Offering at the Distance. She had not dismissed her duty to challenge the emperor, and ordinarily, she would never jeopardise the spiritual cohesion of the three realms of nature by not giving everything of herself to complete her charge to usher in the Aquarian age successfully. But for *once*, she wanted a part of her life to be spontaneous and led by her heart. She was restless to experience falling in love and sharing a life with a human man. She was mature enough, wise enough, and ready to prove herself worthy. Not that she needed to prove anything to anyone because she was the Empress, and regardless of her inner desires, she remained firmly committed to her main charge. But what harm could it do to have a little fun now, rather than at some other sun turn? She was not breaking any rules, not really. Not important ones, anyway. And the unquestionably loyal Awakener would watch over her. It was just a trial, after all.

Bubbling waters and the sound of splashing from within the travel well located at the other end of the dais, along with the strong scent of Raynorlorium, alerted her to the arrival of the Awakener. A glittering, golden orb emerged, shining brightly in the darkened cavern as it rose majestically over the thick stone edge, floated clear of the well, and then lowered to the ground. The orb dimmed, the Awakener stepped out and sent it back to the unseen with a small gesture.

The Awakener was a slender, androgynous being with a pleasant, unruffled air about them. Their skin was a light brown, and their waist-long, silver-black hair smelled faintly of fresh, damp grasses. They walked across the dais to stand beside her and drawing back their hood, turned their long, thin face and bright, curious eyes to the Empress, who had turned to acknowledge their arrival.

"You are determined to progress your plan, Empress?" They asked, in a voice a few octaves deeper than one might expect. It was a rhetorical question, as it was clear by her attire and determined look that she was.

She nodded. "And I command you to help me," she replied before they could begin their pointless objections again.

In stark contrast to Salliniquai's, the Awakener's plain, practical, forest green robe appeared dull and uninteresting until they were outside. Once in the open air, the robe assumed a chameleon-like quality that blended them into their surroundings, and shielded their energy and magic from the fields during their training sessions with her. Usually conceding to the wisdom of the other three teachers, they were strong in their duties and dedication to the Empress. They had already spent a significant amount of time trying to reason with her and dissuade her from going, but in the end, they had to obey her commands, as did the others.

"I wish to try it now before the Elevated One returns." She continued petulantly. She often played up to the Awakener, the only one of her four guardians she could have a bit of fun with, even though her training with them was, by far, the toughest and most dangerous of her lessons. She loved to play tricks on them, affectionately called them her plaything, and enjoyed trying to frustrate them with her antics.

Glancing over, she saw in their expression their divided loyalties towards trying to do their best for her as an independent young woman and for her as an Empress of the True Malsimily. Her attention moved back to the flower portal, as she inwardly acknowledged that the efforts and dedication of the chosen four to support and train her were above exceptional, despite her somewhat trivial grumbles. But fun was out of the question with the Timekeeper. They were far too severe and enigmatic. The Elevated One was all work and no play, and the Alchemist could intuit and sense her energetic state as quickly as they could read their own, which defeated the object of sharing her wickedly teasing sense of humour, as it often went over their head.

As all were clear on the importance of completing her monumental charge, she had had no reason to dish out commands until now. Now, she felt restless and restricted, like her wings had been clipped. She was eager to test her strengths and Empresserial powers in the human physical realm, and this time, *nothing* would stop her.

"The earth's timeline is right to test the qualities of magic and mundane. Have you no faith in me? In my powers?" Her tone was authoritative, and her bright sea-green eyes flashed with challenge.

"We have no doubts regarding one's power in one's own realm, Empress." The Awakener replied patiently, trying not to appear anxious. "But in the human physical realm, you shall have no powers! The human physical realm is not to be trifled with without ..."

"Trifle, you say. *Trifle?* Why I have no intention of trifling. I want to know a full human life as a woman ..." *so I can fall in love with a human man* "... before I progress my charge of ushering in the Aquarian age with the emperor. I know you know the right spell, Awakener." She said stubbornly. "Why do you insist on resisting my command?"

The Awakener could have replied that it was because they were going against the express instructions of the Elevated One, but instead said reluctantly,

"We do know how to initiate travel, yes ... But we do not recommend it." With a slightly pained expression, they added, "We cannot guarantee the outcome due to aspects of the ritual only the Elevated One can perform. Also ..."

"Oh, be *still*, Awakener. I am not looking for guarantees, only life!" She threw back impatiently. "It is my power alone giving support and life to all in the realm, is it not?" She did not wait for an answer but continued as though the Awakener had agreed with her. "I, therefore, *command* you to open the way right now, just for a time." She tilted her head slightly, and her eyes softened as she looked up at them with a manipulative, pleading gaze. "Just enough time for a very short trial at first. Two or three human days. Then, should I succeed and return safely, you can send me back to experience one full life."

The Awakener hesitated. But as they could not refuse the commands of the Empress, they responded submissively, "As you wish, Empress."

A thumbnail-sized symbol of Venus, made of smooth, tiny emeralds, studded the centre of her forehead. Murmuring a brief magical incantation, the Awakener infused this symbol of the feminine, transforming it into its Malsimily nature of transparency. Salliniquai, meanwhile, carefully removed one of the huge, purple petals from the flower standing within the travelling circle of brown earth and laid it just outside the circle.

"There. Placing this here will ensure my return back to you." She said, stepping into the centre of the flower and sitting down within its soft petals. The remaining petals began to close around her, and after a moment or two of quiet stillness, she dropped down through the orangey-brown stem. Like a shooting star, she travelled to the physical human realm. Earth.

Within the geode a few seconds later, the most senior of the four guardians, the Timekeeper, shimmered into the seen beside the Awakener. Raising their heavily ringed hands sedately, they pushed back the hood of their robe. In a smooth monotone, which took on an echoey quality when speaking enigmatically especially, they broke the heavily ominous silence that seemed to fill the geode.

"The Empress has journeyed to the human physical realm?"

The Awakener nodded. "She has. However, the timeline was not aligned with what she had in mind, we had to ..."

"Intercept? Groovy." They interrupted. "This was expected, of course. The Elevated One envisioned a rebellious act such as this. They are the most clued-up being in the history of clued-up beings, ever, when it comes to the behaviour of the Empress." They said in admiration as they hovered a bit closer. "Having pre-empted the current situation, and since she shall have no magical abilities there, we infused the cycle of nine into her timeline as a means of support earlier. It will activate the Hereditary Kee, and once aligned to the human host, visionary and sensory memories shall reveal the nature of the Realm and the Empress."

The Awakener stared at them perplexedly, distracted by their somewhat strange terminology. Groovy? Clued up? What were they talking about?

"But why is this necessary?" They asked after several seconds had passed. The Timekeeper backed away slightly.

"We have reviewed the broader picture. Her knowledge of the three realms of nature shall be ... useful when the Third Way comes forth. Besides, they were small interventions. Their importance shall not be apparent until ... a later date."

The Awakener watched the Timekeeper closely. The two barely perceptible pauses in their explanation were quite unusual. They had never known them to hesitate when explaining before. Either they were holding something back or meant to say something entirely different and then changed their mind. One of those ominous, human physical realm sayings, perhaps? The Awakener was used to this to some degree, for it was true to the enigmatic nature of the Timekeeper.

"We presume these actions were required in this case. As for translating her journey?" The Awakener looked to their companion expectantly.

"It is our responsibility to translate her adventures. Some of the earthy references, strange as they may be, were relatively easy to include, but True Malsimily has no translation. As such, we shall replace the missing text with a close approximation if necessary." The Timekeeper appeared excited by the prospect.

"For ease of human understanding?" the Awakener asked.

"It is as you say." The Timekeeper agreed, their features settling back into their usual stern expression. "Fortunately, we combined the orb energy trigger with the cycle of nine."

"In the three mystical books by the author you have put a spell on, we understand?"

"That is so. The Elevated One worked with us on that particular arrangement." The Timekeeper began to back away. "For the love of the Empress, then." Drawing their hood forwards over their head, they turned and shimmered away.

The Awakener bowed slightly, watching them go. "For the love of the Empress ..."

Guided by the Awakener, who would often allow the Empress to believe they could be manipulated as easily as putty in her hands, an overly smug, confident Salliniquai searched for an appropriate host for her Empresserial energy, unaware that the Elevated One had chosen her trial host for her. It was not the womanly host she was hoping for. No. In their wisdom, her guardians sent her to an unexpected host. A perfect fit for her stubborn, immature ways and the best way to test her skills during her first live taste of humanity.

1

Rowanshire, England. Sunday 1st March, 2020.

Scared out of her wits with her stomach churning sickeningly, Sally was trapped in a dream more frightening than anything she had ever experienced. In the dream, her strained, wretched scream burned her lungs with a stinging force she would never have believed herself capable of expressing, stretching on for so long the pain in her throat reached a breaking point.

The shock of experiencing an endless fall through a black nothingness was the cause. It seemed to go on forever through the oppressive, unfriendly darkness, and she knew it was because of her failure that she was now falling through the unseen—a space within a space with no boundary and no end. She felt a tense disappointment within herself and was terrified of the creature waiting to devour her at the end of her fall.

The air was a chilling, high-pitched whistle rushing past. Tumbling this way and that, she was dizzy beyond belief as her shocking scream pierced the otherwise deadly silent surroundings. Suddenly, a slim glimmer of hope in the form of a faint voice calling her name caught her attention. Although it seemed to be coming from a long way away, it slowed her fall. With every ounce of her will, she latched onto it. Her scream faded then, dwindling painfully away as she gasped herself awake.

Wide-eyed and startled, she lay curled in a ball beneath her bed covers for a long moment. Unable to stop herself from trembling, she willed the dreadful dream to retreat from her mind so her actual surroundings could return and her thoughts make sense again. She closed her eyes then, wanting to languish in her bed's reassuring warmth and familiarity for a few moments longer.

A sudden, inexplicable, spine-tingling chill raced down her back, and she opened her eyes and frowned, immediately anxious. Confusion was evident in her gaze as she realised that immediately after wishing the details of the dream away, she lost all memory of the events of the entire weekend and the details of the dream. Her mind had become strangely empty and, quite worriedly, blank. Thrown by this odd realisation, she was relieved to hear her mother's familiar voice again.

"Sally?"

"Mm ..." she responded groggily.

"Sal?"

"Yeah?" She touched her throat gently, frowning slightly.

"Are you getting up today, hun?" Her mum called through the gap in her open bedroom door. Hearing no reply and seeing no movement from beneath the bedcovers, she rapped the door smartly twice and pushed it fully open. She bustled over to the windows to draw open the curtains. "Morning, hun. I have been calling you for ages. I've never known you to sleep so deeply."

Distracted by her mother's appearance, she yawned, groaned, stretched herself out, and then rubbed at her eyes, which were heavy with sleep. Peeking out from under the covers, she squinted at the silhouetted figure as pale light spilt into the room directly into her face. She had indeed forgotten the dream about playing the deadly game of Snakes and Ladders as she mumbled a lazy,

"Morning, Mum," but her voice was a husky, empty echo.

"You're awake then. Why didn't you answer me?"

"I did. I've lost my voice." Simone glanced at her quickly, then walked over and lightly touched the back of her hand to her forehead. "I'm alright. I'm not sick."

"Let's hope not. You can't come down with a cold the day before we travel."

"I'm alright." She insisted in the loudest whisper she could manage. Then she frowned. "We're going to Saint Lucia tomorrow? But I thought ..."

"Actually, I'm not surprised, especially after all the screaming I heard at the party." Simone interrupted. "You've screamed yourself hoarse before at the Dome as well. Maybe you did it again?"

"Party? What party?" She asked, but Simone did not hear her. She was over at the window looking out. The Dome? She wondered, but could not remember anything about either. Suddenly worried she might be coming down with something that would stop her travelling the next day, she smiled and nodded in response, trying to look healthy, then turned over to face away from the window so her face did not reveal her concerns to her mother in the pale morning light.

"Are you coming to the shops with me?" Simone asked, glancing around the tidy room.

"Um, I'm a bit tired. Do you mind if I don't?" She mumbled hoarsely.

"No, course not. Stay in bed if you like. It's your last chance to shop, though."

"I've got everything I need ... I think." She replied vaguely, folding the duvet down. She rolled over. "Nanny's gonna be alright, isn't she?"

"Of course, she will. Once I'm there to take care of her." Her response was reassuring. "I'll give you a shout when I get back then," she said cheerily, tickling the toes of her now uncovered foot. "A hot drink of honey and lemon might help, babe. I'll put a bag in a cup, and you can make it when the kettle boils ..."

"Hey!" she snorted, snatching her foot back.

She paused at the door and, in a hushed tone, said. "If you put your music on, keep it low, please. Your dad's working in the study."

"Alright." Lifting her hand in a half-hearted wave, she snuggled back under her covers and yawned widely as her mum disappeared out the door, closing it behind her.

***

Simone's thoughts were on her mum, who lived in Saint Lucia, as she headed down the stairs. Twelve days ago, she had stumbled in the street and broke her hip. It was an unfortunate, inconvenient accident since the three had only recently returned from the island after attending a wedding there. Her husband, Richard, had wondered why his wife was responsible for caring for his mother-in-law when several family members lived there. Once she explained that if left to the others, her mum's care would be handled in a slip-shod, hap-hazard manner, with her feeling like she was an inconvenience, he agreed they should go.

"Dad needs me back as soon as possible. Mum needs a lot of

support, which he can't provide, so we have to go." She told him after hearing about the fall. Her mum was not her only concern, however. She wanted to leave England before the new virus she had heard about became a problem.

"I'll book our seats right away then," Richard replied, having also been keeping a close eye on its spread. Acting swiftly, he booked three premium economy seats on open tickets.

Simone wondered if they were overreacting a bit. Other types of Bird flu have circulated the world before. She could not imagine this situation as any worse than those others, and things turned out alright then. Would this time be any different? Their long-time friends, Marvin, and Julianna, would be surprised to see them back in Saint Lucia, and Andrew would be over the moon to have Sally back to hang out with. So, it is all good. If the flu situation did become a worry, it was better to be there in the hot sun than in freezing cold England anyway.

Knowing Sally, who wished she could live in Saint Lucia all the time, could hear them talking, Richard had winked at his wife, wondering aloud whether they should go without her. As expected, she had rushed into the room and adamantly refused to be left behind. Saint Lucia was her favourite place in the world, and since the age of six, she had played with her Saint Lucian friends and relatives every year, as this was where the Vincent-Payne's took their annual summer holiday.

The sleepy town of Soufriere and her grandparent's house was her second favourite place on the island. She felt like a free spirit with lots of open space to grow, laugh, and play when she was there. Not that she did not grow, laugh, and play in England, it was just a different kind of fun.

"I can help look after nanny, Mum. Please don't leave me here alone," she pleaded, believing they were seriously considering leaving her behind. Leaving her at home alone was never an option, of course. Not at her age.

"Alright, Sally," her dad said, "let's hope the school are alright about having this extra time off."

"I'm sure they'll be fine under the circumstances. She can bring her schoolwork with her." Her mum had said, with a quick, reassuring wink in her direction.

And so, her parents had arranged everything. While they were away, their next-door neighbour would take care of Serenity, her cat. Popping in to feed and water her once a day was no inconvenience, and with a cat flap in the back door, she could come and go as she pleased. Since she had often done the same favour for them, it was no biggy.

In her bedroom, a larger-than-average, strangely coloured, perfectly round balloon attached to the knob of her chest of drawers by a long white piece of string drifted in and out of the sunlight filtering in weakly through the window. It bobbed against the ceiling, and as it began to turn, its hazy, silvery purple colours reminded her of something. She could almost grasp it, but then thought, no. That could not possibly be right. She frowned as she stared up at it. It was her orballoon! She hesitated. *Orballoon?* What a strange thing to call it. She had the strangest idea that she and her orballoon had, at some point, changed places, somehow. It was almost like they had... As she watched, the slowly turning balloon revealed two small pictures. One was of a large, smiling face, half covered by a large, wide-brimmed purple hat, and the other, a whole boy. They were vaguely familiar, and the strange thought that she knew them almost as well as her two best friends, Smudge-face, and the Juggernaut, came to her. *But from where?* She closed her eyes again and lay still, thinking. A moment later,

19

she sat bolt upright in bed as disconnected but significant scraps of information popped into her head. The pictures on the orballoon were of Saxon and Noxas. It is the orballoon from ... the party! From the funny-looking clown who had stopped her at the door. She remembered that bit now, but everything else about the weekend was fuzzy-ish. Throwing the bedcovers aside, she got out of bed, crossed the room, and went to stand before the chest of drawers in front of the window. She opened it a few inches to let in some fresh air, then took a deep breath. She felt frustrated as she frowned again, wondering why she could not remember specific details about the weekend clearly.

How could she have forgotten everything!? This wasn't good. What could have happened to make her lose her memory? It could not be some sort of mad coincidence because she remembered going to bed the night before thinking of Saint Lucia. A blow to the head, then? No, it could not be that either, because she remembered their recent trip's details. She remembered being at a wedding party attended by famous people. Not just famous people but famous musicians her mum and dad were friends with, having all grown up on the Cobblestones estate—a homegrown band called Deep Silver Lining, whose members were originally from Rowanshire.

Her parents' first date had been at one of their concerts. They had all their albums and always received VIP tickets when the band played locally. They loved their music and described it as brilliantly thought-provoking. Snowboy, the lead singer, had gifted her a travel guitar that was the perfect size for her. He actually *gave* her a guitar, and then he and keyboard Trevor signed it! Awesome. Right? So, as she could remember those specific details, she knew she wasn't going mad. Could she be experiencing a mental block of some sort? She noticed several cuts and bruises on her body then and wondered whether she had been in an accident, which could have brought on the memory loss. It could have happened that way. She had read about being concussed and had seen it happen to people on the telly. But if that were the case, how come her mum was not acting differently towards her? No, this was something else. She sighed. Something strange was happening here, and not knowing what was frustrating.

Sally had no idea that she had been hosting the energy of Empress Salliniquai over the weekend, and had taken part in an exciting but dangerous trial.

Leaning on her windowsill with her chin resting in her hands, she watched a couple of cyclists walking their bikes through the estate, their wheels making tracks in the snow. She bit her lip, deep in thought. As hard as she tried, she could not remember any further details. Wracking her brain with such a puzzle would eventually drive her up the wall. Nothing about the situation made sense. How could she get to the bottom of this?

Deciding the situation was way beyond her own common-sense abilities, she thought of her two best friends. They would help her remember. Without them, she would have no chance of figuring things out, not with her usual, dithery-like way of thinking. Her thoughts were more settled when they were around. She would have been with them, after all. They could help her piece together the weekend's events and unravel the mystery of her memory loss.

She felt an urgent, throbbing sensation on her left thigh and a sharp stab of pain on her foot, close to her right heel, both of which had begun to pulse painfully the longer she stood up. She pushed the waist of her pyjama bottoms down and gasped when she discovered a long, rasp-like scrape on her thigh. There were several bruises down her arms and legs, her shoulders felt unusually stiff, a couple of blisters on the pads of one of her hands ached, and two of her fingers were slightly swollen. *I don't understand this. Just what did we get up to?* She wondered, twisting her pursed lips in confusion and uncertainty. Putting aside the strange injuries and sensations for the moment, she reached up and gently stroked her fingers down the smooth skin of the balloon. Unexpectedly, it burst with a loud bang as she did so, sending the essence of the Empress Salliniquai back to the Realm of the Empress, taking the four lesser lesson kees which remained a part of her sacrificial charge with it.

Surprised, Sally jumped back with her hand flat against her chest as an unexpected ripple of heat rose through her, and she trembled and gasped at the strange sensation that was both weird and welcome. As Empress Salliniquai's energy had left her when the balloon burst, the Hereditary Kee, now fully infused, had taken hold within her.

Moving backwards slowly, she drew in a sharp, hissing breath, wincing at the sting in her heel as she returned to the bedside. When the backs of her legs touched the bed, she dropped onto it, then began chewing on a fingernail, again thoughtful.

"Sally? What was that?" Her dad called from the study. *God Bless the mothers*, one of his favourite songs by Deep Silver Lining, played in the background, the sound of the lead singers sultry voice was soulful, poignant, and non-intrusive.

"It's alright, Dad. My orballoon burst, that's all."

"Sally?"

She left the room and stood at the top of the stairs where he could see her. She mouthed the words *I have lost my voice.*

"Oh. Yes. Your mum said. What are you up to?" He asked in a mildly suspicious tone.

"Nothing! Sorry. My Orballoon burst." She thought of her friends again. "Can I invite my mates around this morning to study? We won't be noisy, I promise." She added quickly, as loud as she could whisper.

"Yes, alright ..." His voice grew faint as he turned away from the doorway; his attention returned to his business inside. He did not hear her response.

"Thanks," she replied hoarsely. She returned to her room and lay back down on the bed. Her brow wrinkled again as she glanced at the jagged balloon pieces on the floor, then looked to the window as she heard the familiar sound of Serenity's bell collar. As the cat meandered in, she speculated as to whether she was returning from a night out prowling around in the dark, or from an early morning hunt.

Taking her usual route to the bed, the cat picked her way between the contents of the dresser, leapt down onto the chair, padded across the floor, and then jumped up onto the bed. Her wet paws left faint track marks as she snuggled into the rumpled duvet.

"Thanks, Serenity," she scolded the cat mildly in a whisper. Then, her eyes fixed on her collar. *Serenity's collar!* It saved me from ...? But the memory danced away before she could fully grasp it. "Oh, why can't I remember!" She fumed, slamming her hands down on the bed on either side of her. She winced as the one with the swollen fingers, throbbed, then looked towards the now startled cat, standing stiff and ready to bolt. "Sorry ..." She stroked the cat reassuringly, and her familiar touch calmed her at once.

After a moment, she reached for her phone and opened her contacts. She spoke to the Juggernaut first, making an offer she knew her friend could not refuse.

"Come for a second breakfast, Juggs. I need a favour." Then she called Smudge-Face. "I need you, girlfriend. How soon can you get here?"

"Give me half an hour."

"Cool. See you then." She had to shout whisper that she had lost her voice and the call was not a prank to them both before they would take her seriously. All three had fallen foul of prank calls in the past.

While waiting for her friends to arrive, she thought of all the great things she would enjoy again when she returned to Saint Lucia the next day. She could lie on her bed for hours staring through the window, up at the sky, imagining she was there. Going back was not inconvenient. She was pleased to be going and eager to get back there. She loved telling her friends about her exciting adventures, and as thoughts of everything she was looking forward to came to mind, she hugged herself with joy, glad to be going back. She would get to hang out with her best friend Andrew and his two cute puppies again, and she might go back a third time if they went back in the summer. She sighed softly, a much calmer expression on her face now. Her features softened further when she thought of Andrew. She wondered whether she should tell her friends about the kiss and the question he had asked her before she left, then decided against it. No. She would do so when she had decided on the answer she would give him.

Her suitcase, packed and stored with the others downstairs, was ready for their early morning departure. She was returning to the sun, and it would be brilliant!! She gushed inwardly. With a satisfied sigh and having forgotten about her memory loss for the moment, she leaned back against her headboard, thinking about the things she liked most about Saint Lucia.

She knew loads about the island, known to most adults as the

Jewel of the Caribbean. It was the top wedding and honeymoon destination in the whole wide world and an exotic paradise compared to England, she had bragged enthusiastically to her friends. There were tons of beaches, hidden coves, and shallow bays where the crystal-clear water was cool, and the sand was soft and warm underfoot. You could swim all day, have a beach BBQ, eat fluffy fried bakes, drink ice-cold icicles, enjoy mango-flavoured ice cream, and sunbathe.

It was a safe place for children, so her mum and dad did not have to constantly wonder what she was getting up to or watch her every move. It was good fun hanging out with the local kids all day and late into the evenings, and her parents trusted her and the kids she hung out with to be responsible when getting into their island adventures.

As a third-world country, Saint Lucia relied heavily on the tourist industry and had a robust expat population. As such, there were decent supermarkets, several small malls, and other big shops in the capital and other areas, along with big hotels and all kinds of different businesses, large and small, from restaurants to local food outlets based in cobbled together huts, and from big, flashy bars, to tiny little rum shops which were little more than a shack, with a rough counter for a bar.

For the last five years, while her parents were engaged in lovey-dovey things during their two weeks of quality time together, she spent those two weeks at Andrew's. His house was on a different part of the island close to the airport, in the Lavender Valley. It was totally her favourite place on the island mostly because they had a swimming pool. Staying at his house was way better than any packed-out-to-the-max, flashy hotel.

The two spent much of their time playing *guess where they were going* as they watched the planes take off, then tried to identify the coloured flag on their tails, straining to see them through their cheap binoculars. They also enjoyed horse riding as a neighbour down the road owned the stables in the next bay. Visiting the horses almost daily, they brought them treats such as apples and sugar. Her friends back in England were well jealous of the exotic, long-haul holiday the Vincent-Paynes enjoyed for four weeks every year. They, and Hannah's sister Melissa, were always impressed by the hairstyle she returned with, compliments of Skitter, a reputable beautician, as well as hearing about her exciting adventures, the details of which she would regale them with for hours on her return.

So, back to the mystery of her memory loss and crusty voice. Remembering all this proved she had not suffered any permanent brain damage. Once her friends arrived, they would figure out what happened over the weekend and why she could not remember it. They usually managed to work things out between them. The three were a great team. Even her dad thought so.

Richard thought their daughter was the linchpin of the trio of young girls, calling her the balancing element in their three-way friendship. When she thought about it later, she saw he had a point. The Juggernaut, for example, was a bolshy, outspoken, often tactless girl with the single-minded goal of becoming an Olympic champion. Tall, long-limbed, and gangly, she was always up for anything, provided it did not interfere with her training schedule, and as a Leo, she was a loyal friend. Whenever she spoke of her future, she always began the sentence with ... *When I am an Olympic medallist ...*

At school, she was the pride of their year when it came to sports, and in her first year, she successfully won her way onto the school under fourteen's netball, hockey, and swim teams. Her parents had won several awards, medals, and trophies for their sporting efforts, and she was determined to follow in their footsteps. Although they had not gained an Olympic standard themselves, she had grown up on their accomplishments and now, similarly, strived towards becoming a sporting champion. The athletics idea had taken hold just after her tenth birthday, when she discovered she did not have to choose just one or two specialities; but could do ten if she were a decathlete. The world of athletics had become her favourite sport, even though she had been told many times that there was no decathlete competition for women.

"There might be by the time I'm ready to compete," she threw back immediately. Professing that, "Seven sports are not enough to satisfy me." But she would settle for the heptathlon if she had to, for now. Once she turned twelve, she joined the best athletics club in Rowanshire, eager and ambitious to get started on her Olympic career. With a natural love of all sporting endeavours and an early recognised talent as a potential professional sportswoman, she was earmarked for great things. Her life had a singular purpose, and with her natural talent for sports, her desire to fulfil her ambition looked promising.

Smudge-face, a bright girl with a friendly, bubbly nature, could not be more different than the Juggernaut. An easy-going and dreamy Piscean, she was very obsessive about her art. She had a quiet, sometimes wary disposition around strangers and was happy so long as she could express herself freely through her painting. She was talented in the way she saw things with her arty eyes. Her unique lens often confused her friends when she spoke of things in their environment with her artistic flavour. Whatever vision she saw and drew from memory became a colourful creation on the page before her, and her friends were impressed and proud of her exceptional talent.

So, what her dad said about them could be true, as their interests were so different. Their friendship was built on trust and loyalty born out of knowing each other all their lives and their parents being friends for most of their lives. The girls bounced off each other nicely with their lively, seemingly unending energy, mix of talents, interests, impulses, and ambitions. They were also incredibly mature for their age.

The three girls spent most of their free time hanging out at Sally's house, which was a neutral place compared to their homes. The Juggernaut's house was generally quiet, but her bedroom was always untidy, with various sports kits and stuff lying around, which one could trip over. On the other hand, Smudge-face's house was always noisy and exciting, with family members interrupting and busying about. Whenever they spent time in her loft room, which was huge with a long window the length of the room, she always came away with some smudge or stain on her clothes, so she was glad they usually hung out at hers.

The girls took turns hosting sleepovers at their respective houses often, at least once a month. They were always lively when they arranged a sleepover at Smudge-face's house. Her dad, Roger, was a senior fireman, and her mum, Avilone, was the Chief Executive of a small children's charity and shop. Her fourteen-year-old twin brothers, Dyon, and Douglas, were boisterous, teasing, pranksters. But generally, only with each other. They loved playing on their PlayStation, and when they got going, they could hear them arguing and fighting about who was cheating or losing from her room above.

"Oi, you jammy sod!" or "Hey, that's cheating!!" They would exclaim loudly.

On some of their sleepovers, the boys liked playing board games too and held knockout competitions with herself and the

28

Juggernaut if Smudge-face was in a particularly obsessive painting mood. Her older sister, Melissa, was eighteen years old, and worked weekends at her aunt's salon while studying a course in Hairdressing and Salon Management at the local college. With ambitions of opening her own salon one day, she had been practising on the three girls for years, trying out simple, traditional, or sometimes quite elaborate hairstyles on them.

"Not a hairdresser," she would state in case the girls forgot the difference in status. "But a hairstylist." Followed by her usual boast, "When Aunty Janet takes me on full-time next year, I'm gonna be better than any of the other trainee stylists in the place. By then, I'll be skilled in working with all hair types." It was usually hair extensions of some kind on Smudge-face. Corn rows and twists on Sally, and a complicated blow dry or a style using oversized curlers or sponge ties on the Juggernaut, who usually wore her hair in a scruffy, hastily tied pony or a simple plait down her back. Of course, there had been a few disasters, but she had quickly rectified them, and the girls continued to trust her with their hair. "It's criminal what you subject your hair to, Juggs." She would sigh whenever she was working on her long, thick, gingery-blonde tresses. "All that chlorine from swimming will irreparably damage your hair. You are still using the shampoo and conditioner I recommended, yeah? It's literally your only protection from regular exposure to those harsh chemicals."

"I am Mel, I promise. I don't want to end up with limp, ratty hair, either. Since you recommended that shampoo, I use it religiously."

"Excellent. Good girl."

Whenever they stayed at hers, a condition of their sleepover was watching an educational documentary. This was cool with her because she loved them. She had grown up watching documentaries with her mum and dad and had three favourite presenters she could watch repeatedly. David Dimbleby, presenting The Seven Ages of Britain and The Picture of Britain. Everything David Attenborough presented and produced on nature and the protection of nature, and then, as she was interested in astrology, and astronomy, topics not taught in school, Carl Sagan's Cosmos, on the nature of the universe and planets. These were not the common, AI-generated programmes of perfection most of her age group would be interested in watching these days. Fast-paced and overly exciting, with special effects and such.

Her mum and dad, who knew everything, said she would probably learn more from watching those documentaries than in certain school classes. As far as she was concerned, the programmes she liked were way more interesting than some of the subjects at school and portrayed more accurate accounts of history and provided information on how all living creatures survived in the world. Overall, she was a good student at the top of her class with a keen intelligence, respect for authority, and broad interests.

She was the linchpin for her parents as well. A position she liked to feel was true, being their only child and that. Not that they needed a linchpin at all because they were always so lovey-dovey; it was embarrassing. Still, if there was such a thing, she was it, just as she was with her two best friends who, incidentally, have the real names of Hope and Hannah, respectively.

Having made her two phone calls, she threw away the balloon scraps, washed, dressed, and then prepared a jug of juice and enough toast to feed the five thousand. Back on her bed, licking butter off her fingers, she reached across to her bedside table and opened the single drawer. She took out the unique little book, appropriated from Hannah's mum's charity shop during the summer holidays, and opened it. The cover was fascinating and lovely, with a strange, smoky appearance and a secret element that (*True Malsimily, translation unavailable*). Looking at it now, it had changed quite dramatically. There seemed to be another mysterious element to it she could somehow visualise and read, but which (*True Malsimily, translation unavailable*). Instinctively, she understood that others could not see this magical quality because neither of her friends had mentioned it when she had shown it to them in the shop. The book resonated with her especially, bringing with it a deep hope she had not realised she had until she picked it up. It was the hope that all would become right and fair in the world in time.

Fully awake now, she felt an inexplicable, undeniable shift within her, along with a sudden clarity. The subtle widening of her perspective after her mysterious adventure was the start of her maturity into adulthood. Wasn't it amazing how a new experience could change one's mind about something they were initially absolutely convinced of? Recognising a new line of thinking, for example. Over the weekend, she had somehow discovered a new aspect of life that was impossible to reverse or dismiss. It was a magically enhanced, monumental series of events that enhanced her spiritual integrity, imagination, intellect, and determination, which would now change her life.

In the magical Realm of the Empress...

"She won't believe it to be just some sort of *mad coincidence*." The Timekeeper remarked confidently. "This girl is smart. An exemplary choice, Elevated One." They bowed slightly; their misty form shifting ethereally. "We shall disperse now to attend the Awakener." Pulling their hood up to cover their head, they turned and shimmered away. The Elevated One watched them go again with a curious look in their eyes.

In the human physical realm...

Sally was considering the book's cover when she heard the front door, which she had left on the latch, bang open. Returning the book to the drawer, she cringed slightly at the sound of the Juggernaut's heavy footsteps. Good grief! Trust her to come barging in. She should have said to come in quietly, she thought belatedly.

Hope, aka the Juggernaut, was indeed the first to arrive. Her fresh, freckled face had a healthy glow, and her untidy, gingery-blonde hair was still damp after spending an hour at the gym. She immediately helped herself to a piece of toast and enthusiastically began to tuck in. Sitting on the bed, she scooted back to lean against the wall and stroked a hand none too gently down Serenity's back. She lightened her touch considerably when Serenity hissed and threw an irritated gaze her way. As a girl with seemingly untold energy, Hope did everything enthusiastically.

"So, what's up, Bubblelicious?" She asked, then grinned. "Mum and Dad were well impressed with those radical pics you sent me. The ones with you and Snowboy, especially. I've literally only just gotten round to showing them."

Hope's parents, William, and Daphne Hallerton, were introduced by Simone at an annual sporting conference years ago. All three got up every morning at 5.30 am to go to the gym, followed by a hearty breakfast, and then all left for work or school. Hope was looking forward to adding extra training sessions to her busy schedule now that she had enrolled in the sports academy. She had far to go, beginning with competing against other schools on sports day, then competing at the county level, then at the district level and as she got older, at national and international levels, followed inevitably by the Olympics. It was her dream, she expected to be the best, and she talked of nothing else.

"So, how did you lose your voice?" Before she could answer, the sound of light, running footsteps coming up the stairs announced the arrival of Hannah, aka Smudge-face. A petite, quirky girl of West Indian origins. She entered the bedroom and immediately flung herself into the wide, wicker seat on the other side of the bedside unit. Laying her large art bag on the floor beside her, she poured herself a beaker of juice.

"Hiya Hope. What's the emergency, Sal? I hope we can solve whatever mystery this is before you jet off tomorrow, you lucky thing. I'm sooo jealous." She grumbled enviously.

Hannah had been drawing and painting for as long as Sally had known her and was extremely gifted at it. She had the most fantastic eye for detail, especially with faces, was never without her sketch pad and drawing essentials, and her fingertips often had smudges on them.

When the three girls discussed their career dreams, as they often did, all agreed that Hannah would one day be a famous artist with her own studio or some architectural designer of fabulously strange, quirky buildings. It was clear to all that she was another very talented girl with a great future ahead of her.

Realising their seven-year-old was obsessed with painting, Roger and Avilone Alexander knew Hannah's interest in art was here to stay. They cleared out the loft and moved her bedroom up there, giving her more space to spread her art paraphernalia around and reducing the risk of having paint smudges and whatnot on the walls and surfaces all over the house.

Her parents provided her with supplies from colouring books and sketch pads to paint pallets and easels. She was a member of the school art club, subscribed to a junior art magazine, and had two of her sketches on display at the school's annual junior exhibition since they began their first year of secondary school. She would attend a school of art for ten days in the summer holidays and was looking forward to it.

Sally's two best friends were not just talented in their chosen fields, they were very close to being child geniuses, and both demonstrated great ambition, determination, drive, and a maturity way beyond their years that would keep them true to their dreams.

With the trio of best friends now complete, she got off the bed, walked over to the door and closed it. Turning to them with a look of uncertain puzzlement, she explained her predicament in a loud, forced whisper.

"Something strange ... I mean ... something scary has happened, apart from losing my voice, I mean. I can't remember what happened over the weekend." She said her tone serious. The two girls looked at her blankly for a moment. Hope was chewing on a piece of toast, and Hannah had stopped rummaging in her bag to look up at her as she returned to the bed. "And I think funny dreams, which felt real somehow, might have something to do with it. It's driving me mad." She sighed heavily. Her friends exchanged a puzzled look. "To jog my memory, can you explain what we did from the time we left school on Friday?" Her gaze shifted between the two. "Hannah, you're good with details ..."

"You've forgotten *everything?!* The weekend was beyond radical!" Exclaimed Hope. "... even though we almost got into trouble because you met us late in the park." She reached for more toast. "It was a totally wicked weekend, Sal."

"What do you mean when you say your dreams felt real?" Hannah asked, getting straight to the most unusual point she had made. Her large, almond eyes, with their curious gaze, were fixed on her friend.

"I've had a few flashbacks, but it's all mixed up. Some of it doesn't make sense, and then, there's these ..." she pulled back her sleeves to show them her arms, then lifted the hem of the long skirt she'd put on to show them her leg. The girls went to her and bent close for a better look. The three exchanged troubled glances. "I need to know how I got these." Wincing a little, she sat back, crossed her legs beneath her, and then pulled a large, yellow smiley-faced emoji cushion onto her lap.

"You look like I do after a tough week of hockey and netball practice." Hope chuckled, tickling Serenity under her chin gently. Hannah glanced at her with her eyebrows arched as she returned to her seat.

"Okay, well, we were together practically the whole time from Friday after school, weren't we, Hope? I don't remember doing anything that would cause those bruises, though. They look painful," she added.

"Yeah, I thought you'd say that." Sally sighed ruefully. "I'm not sure, but I think they happened during the night when I was dreaming, and yeah, they do hurt, but not enough to tell my parents or anything."

"What?" Hope's attention returned to her. "How could you get hurt in a dream? Unless you were sleepwalking and fell down the stairs or something." She continued nibbling on her slice of toast.

"Possible, I suppose, but unlikely because neither my mum or dad mentioned anything about a fall down the stairs."

"Don't worry, Bubbs; we'll get to the bottom of it. I am quite intrigued myself now," said Hannah. "What's the last thing you remember?" she asked calmly.

Sally closed her eyes and took a deep breath, glad her two best friends were with her as she tried to recall the weekend's events. Together they would find the answers when they picked apart the details. With familiar things around her, she was a little more relaxed, comfortable, and ready to sort out ... whatever needed sorting out. She opened her eyes again and began to tell her story...

***

Yes, she was late meeting them at the park on Friday morning because on her way out of her bedroom, out of the corner of her eye, she thought she saw the image on the front cover of her unique little book, The serenity Experience, shift and expand. She was about to look closer when she noticed the time. She left this part out of her explanation, however. There was no need to distract them with the mysterious nature of her special book.

"You're gonna be late, Sally." Her mum had called up from the bottom of the stairs, prompting her to hurry her departure.

"I remember grabbing my schoolbag, thinking I was boringly average compared to you two, and wishing I knew what I was really, really good at."

"You're good at blowing the biggest bubble-gum bubbles in the history of big bubbles, ever. That's something, at least." Hope said glibly. Hannah chuckled while Sally ignored her, shaking her head dismissively. The gap between her two front teeth, which occasionally caused her to lisp, was a great advantage when blowing bubble-gum bubbles, according to Hope.

"Be careful what you wish for," Hannah commented lightly. It was just the sort of thing she would say.

"So, on Friday," she continued. "After the school bell, I grabbed my stuff and then went to meet you two."

"We met in the hall, remember?" Hannah prompted, chewing on a second piece of toast. Her drawing pad was open and prepared on her lap.

2

Friday 28th February, 2020.

At the sound of the school bell, she had gathered up her things, picked up her bag from the floor beside her desk and made her way out into the hall with the other girls from the class. Unwrapping a piece of bubble gum retrieved from her blazer pocket, she welcomed the strong flavour as it burst richly around her mouth. She was addicted to bubble gum; and everyone knew her for constantly chewing a piece. Almost immediately, Hannah fell into step beside her, and the two girls continued down the long hall among the crowd of other students, all making their way noisily out into the bright afternoon, occasionally calling.

"See you Monday," or "See you later" to their friends. They reached the place where the three usually met and huddled together to wait for Hope.

"I'm so excited about my dinner party tonight!" Hannah gushed, her happiness evident in her bright eyes and restless gaze. "Now we're all the same age; Hope will have to stop going on about my not yet being a teenager." She bounced up and down on the balls of her feet impatiently, then stood on tiptoe, trying to see over the heads of the other students, her gaze shifting from one set of doors to another.

Sally laughed and rolled her eyes as she hooked her arm through her friend's.

"Excited! No, really?! It's not like it's all you've talked about for the last month or anything." She glanced back over her shoulder towards the school's main double doors. "Can you see her yet? My mum said she'd wait for us by the ... oh look, there she is." They both waved a hurry-up gesture to their friend, then began strolling towards the gates, giving her time to catch up to them.

"Tonight's the night, girlfriend." Hannah gushed again.

"Nooo, really!?" She repeated, dragging out her words. "You're like an over-excited three-year-old."

"Ha, ha, ha, very funny." The old quip was not amusing however.

"What's funny, Smudge-Face?" Hope asked, coming up behind them and draping her arms over their shoulders. Towering over Hannah, she almost knocked her over as her large sports bag fell off her shoulder and whacked into her back.

"Hey, watch it, Juggernaut." Hannah cried, annoyed. Used to the strong, powerful nickname, Hope grinned.

"Okay, now that the most important member of our little trio has arrived; let's go disco," she ordered, in her usual, take-charge manner. Shifting her bag to her other shoulder, she moved around to the other side of Sally to link their arms.

Walking quicker, they hurried along amongst the hundreds of

other school girls, chatting, laughing, and heading towards the gates, eager to be off school grounds. The three were an odd little group at school, accepted by most, kept at arm's length by others—a trio on the periphery of the usual cliques and gangs.

"Are you sure your birthday isn't tomorrow, Smudge-face? Maybe you were really born on the twenty-ninth of February and are literally only three-and-a-half years old, tiny little thing that you are." Suggested Hope, grinning broadly again.

"Nope, it's definitely my thirteenth birthday today," countered Hannah proudly, rising to the bait. "I made the twenty-eighth by the skin of my teeth."

"Or by the sweat of your mum's labour," Hope chuckled.

"... and I've been saved from being teased for the rest of my schoolgirl life for being a three-year-old." She continued, as they came upon the school gates.

"We know the math." Her friends replied in unison flatly—their usual response to the running joke of Hannah's age.

Hannah had initially refused the idea of a party in the afternoon, claiming that thirteen was too old for that sort of thing. "Can a few of my friends come for tea after school instead?" She had asked.

"I don't see why not. Maybe in fancy dress?" Her mum suggested. "Just to make it a bit more fun. We can say it is a dinner party rather than a tea party?"

"Um ..." She was undecided.

"It sounds a lot more grown up, Han." She added persuasively.

"Hmm ... yeah, alright. A dinner party it is."

"With a buffet dinner?" added her dad. "Others will come a few hours later. Feeding them all will be easier to manage if they can help themselves. That sound alright, Han?"

"Yep. Cool and the gang." He chuckled at the phrase he often used himself, liking that Hannah and her friends had adopted it too, even though they were unfamiliar with the eighties disco band.

The girls were in good spirits. School was over, and the weekend the three had been eagerly waiting for had finally arrived. They had been looking forward to Hannah's Heroine-themed Pizza Dinner Party for weeks, especially since she had promised all sorts of shenanigans, and boys, meaning her brothers, who half of the older girls at their school fancied.

"There'll be lots of grub and a two-tiered, chocolate-orange birthday cake." She had promised. "And although Mel isn't staying, she's gonna take a few pictures so I can do a painting afterwards."

Usually, at this time of year, England would be going through a cold snap, with the worst part of the winter season upon them. Fortunately, on this day, the weather had been unseasonably mild and would continue to be so for a day or two, or so the forecasters had confidently predicted. Which meant the dinner party could be held outside in the garden, under a gazebo. Hannah always complained about having to spend her birthday shivering. She was delighted to be graced with such mild weather, for once.

She invited ten of her school friends, including Sally and Hope, to her Heroine themed, Pizza Dinner Party, and once they left, family and friends would turn the event into a proper house party, and the grown-ups would take over, boogying away to their old school music. She and her cousins would hang out at the top of the stairs instead of going to bed, badgering their older brothers, sisters, and cousins into sneaking the odd soft drink or snack up to them whilst the adults partied late into the night below.

Hope's eyes lit up when she saw it was Simone waiting by the car.

"Fantastic!" She exclaimed. "It's your mum. Very cool and the gang, Bubblelicious." She gave her arm a firm squeeze.

"Uh-huh," Sally responded, wincing a little at her tight grip. She blew a large, pink bubble with her gum, popped it, and then licked the sticky sweetness around her mouth, relishing the strawberry flavour. She exchanged a knowing look with Hannah. Hope would race to sit in the front seat to chat with her mum on the way home, not about Hannah's Heroine-themed Pizza Dinner Party but about sports and athletics because Simone was a sports coach.

Back in her bedroom, she continued hoarsely ...

"Of the party, I remember arriving at your house, Han," she reached for a piece of toast which was now cold and soggy but still nice as it was practically drowning in butter. "Where we changed into our party clothes and ..."

"To jog your memory, we should start with something easy. Do you remember what you changed into?" Hope interrupted, reaching for another piece of toast. She offered a scrap to Serenity, who sniffed it with disinterest, then lowered her head back onto her paws.

They had reached Hannah's home in ten minutes, and the three girls hurried from the car and straight into the house. After removing their shoes at the door, flinging a collective greeting over their shoulders to Hannah's parents, who were busy preparing the table, setting up the gazebo, and laying out all the grub for the party, they had rushed up the stairs to her loft room to get ready.

"I seem to remember ... yeah, I dressed in my all-in-one, black and brown, faux leather Cat woman outfit."

"That's right."

She chose Cat Woman because she adored cats and loved every portrayal of Cat Woman she had seen so far. At the stay-up-late-night sleepover on her thirteenth birthday, her parents had agreed the three films she and her friends could stay up to watch. Batman Returns, the nineties version, with Michelle Pfeiffer playing Cat Woman. How to train your Dragon. An entertaining, animated film, and Cat woman, with Halle Berry. While Smudge-face favoured Halle, and the Juggernaut preferred Michelle in their roles as Cat women, she could not decide who she thought portrayed the role best. A streak of indecisiveness that was totally Libran, according to her book on astrological signs. To her, both were equally badass women Avengers.

Whenever she was at gym club, nimbly dancing with ribbons or along the bench or beam, she thought of how light and graceful her cat's movements were and tried to copy them. Thinking of her cat often gave her confidence and comfort, especially during a practice session.

When Serenity nimbly padded across the backs of chairs, the high back fence at the end of the garden or across the stair railing, head and tail held high and her little paws taking small, close steps, she was always perfectly balanced. Sally sought to copy her balanced elegance. At other times, when she was lazing about daydreaming, she loved it when Serenity curled up in her lap, purring away or asleep, while she gently stroked her back. She was so soothing to be around, always slept so soundly and yet, should she hear a suspicious, unfamiliar sound, her ears would prick back, her eyes would open, and her head would lift inquiringly, putting her at the ready to pounce on any insect or other tiny intruder fool enough to invade her mistress's human domain. She smiled at the thought, then turned her attention back to the day of the party.

Hope, to no one's surprise, had dressed in one of her many tracksuits with a fake, oversized Olympic medal around her neck, while Hannah, also unsurprisingly, dressed up as an artist. Her costume was a wide, paint-smeared apron over a tank top, a long gipsy skirt, and flip-flops.

"I thought I might be a bit overdressed when I saw what you two were wearing," she said self-consciously. "Your outfits didn't look much different to the clothes you normally wear."

"What about the costumes the others were wearing? Do you remember them?" Hannah asked, adjusting the angle of her sketchbook across her lap.

Sally was relieved when the other guests arrived and she could compare their outfits. All had dressed in costumes of strong, famous, no-nonsense heroines such as an Amazon warrior woman, a Viking Valkyrie, and a Cow-girl, complete with a lasso, cowboy hat and chaps. One guest had dressed as an Angel, complete with a halo and wings, looking cool rather than childish. Another guest was dressed as the good witch Maleficent, while another had come as a hedge-witch, dressed in shades of green complete with a tall, pointy hat and a long, green cloak. The last guest dressed as Lieutenant Uhura, the communications officer from Star Trek, and finally, Dyon and Douglas appeared dressed as the Men in Black, complete with sunglasses, black suits, and water pistols. They began squirting the girls with water as soon as they arrived, and their screams were ear-piercing as they dashed about, chased around the garden. It had been a great party, she now remembered.

Later, as the time for her friends to leave drew near, more than two dozen relatives and friends of the family arrived. The adults took over the party, and soon the house was full of people, loud music, clinking glasses and laughter. A mixture of screams and piercing shouts from Hannah's school friends, joined by other kids related to the family, could be heard over calls of,

"Don't forget to take a goodie bag." From Hannah's dad repeatedly, as everyone continued to run around enjoying themselves. The three chaperones, various parents who had arrived earlier, were struggling to stop the kids playing so they could get them ready to go. While Hannah was busy being the centre of attention and Hope battled Dyon on PlayStation, Simone had turned her around and shoo-d her towards the front door.

"Did you thank the Alexanders and say goodbye to Hannah? Where is your school bag?" she asked.

"Yep. I said goodbye and thanked everyone. It's over there by the presents. I can collect it tomorrow. Oh, I didn't get a goodie bag!" She exclaimed, heading back into the lounge. Simone's restraining hand on her shoulder stopped her.

"I'll get that for you and your school bag. Go find your coat, then meet me by the front door, alright?"

"OK," she agreed reluctantly, unable to tear her gaze away from her friends still hanging around the now crowded lounge, dining area and garden. She had just reached the open front door when a rather flamboyantly dressed clown stepped in front of her, barring her way.

"You! I choose you." He bellowed, holding out a gloved hand to offer her the most fabulously coloured balloon she had ever seen. Smiling widely, he gazed at her with a mischievous, sideways glance, then tipped her a friendly wink. Startled by this loud declaration, she glanced around, expecting to find everyone staring at them, but no one was paying her or the clown any attention.

"Oh, um. Thanks, Mr Clown," she replied, looking up at the clown's heavily made-up face. "What sort of clown are you? Did you just get here? How come you arrived so late?" she asked curiously, wondering why Hannah had not mentioned a clown attending. Clowns were for little kids' parties anyway. No self-respecting thirteen-year-old would have a clown at their party.

"Me? Why, I am a smart clown, Sally. Not like the traditional clowns, the ones at little kids' parties, I mean." He replied in a stage whisper behind his hand as he leaned down towards her. "No, I am a Leap Year clown. I appear on on this date on all leap years to issue one extraordinary invitation to the one who has shown themselves to be courageous, quick-witted, strong, and clever. To the one who, in the future, shall be remembered for their contributions to the welfare of the world, literally." His voice lowered, and he sounded a bit sad for a moment. "As such, this is the last time I shall be tasked to search for the latest star, that being yourself, of course."

"Me?" she gasped softly, taken aback.

"Yes, you," he insisted. "I've found many smart, grown-up youngsters like you, Sally." He said, in a camp, sing-songy voice. Straightening up again, he looked her over from her head to her toes. Seemingly satisfied with his inspection, he glanced at her out of the corner of his eye and squinted a little. "It appears I've arrived just in time, Empress."

While the clown spoke, Sally's studiously assessing gaze checked him out from top to bottom. He had the usual false red nose and clown make-up but wore a funky, long black waistcoat that flared out when he moved, showing a bright orange lining. Underneath that, he wore an orange shirt with a ruffled front and ruffled sleeves, baggy black jodhpurs, and a bright orange bowler hat. She liked him, inwardly agreeing with his statement that he was not the usual type of clown. He was wearing one of her favourite colours too, orange.

"Empress? What do you mean, Empress?" she asked after a moment.

The clown bobbed his head, seemingly in reply to her thought. "Why, thank you. It is my favourite colour too and oh, my bad. I meant to say I arrived in time for you to *Impress*." His focused gaze lingered on her as he shook the balloon almost impatiently in her face. "Take it, and good luck at the party!" *So, whilst hosted in a human body, the memory of her true nature escapes her.* Thought the clown.

Sally's expression was slightly suspicious as she reached out and took the offered string. She stared up at the large, perfectly circular balloon, again noting its unusually mixed purple and silver colours which seemed to meld into each other, as it floated above her head, bouncing against the top of the doorframe.

"Balloons are for kids too ... although this one ... is ... very pretty ..." she mused distractedly. Her mum returned to her side then and leaving the noise and kerfuffle of the celebration behind, they stepped outside.

"Hey, mum! Look at this. Have you ever seen such lovely colours on an orballoon before?!" She asked, completely enthralled. With a guiding hand on her shoulder, Simone steered her around the other departing youngsters bunched just outside the door. It was hard for them to converse clearly, over the din. "What did the clown mean by wishing me good luck?"

"Mr Brown? I don't know, hun," she replied distractedly. "Maybe it's his way of saying goodbye." Her mind was on the topic the adults had been discussing during the dinner party. The loveliness of Sally's purple and silver balloon was the last thing on her mind.

When Sally drew the balloon down by its string, she noticed two printed pictures on it. One was the figure of a cheeky-looking boy, laughing. By the way his eyes were squeezed closed and the rest of his body positioned, it was clear he was laughing so hard he was holding his sides to stop them from splitting. The other was the head of a smiling fellow wearing a huge purple hat with a wide, floppy brim. The brim was so large only his chin and smiling mouth showed beneath the rounded curve. Both were about six inches in diameter and curved around the balloon's surface.

"I've never seen an orballoon like this one, mum. Obviously, I'm way too old now for such childish things, but ... I think ... it must be one-of-a-kind. I don't see any others with an orballoon like this one, not even Hannah. And that strange, funny clown wished me luck at the party and then said ... oh, he's gone now," she said, looking over her shoulder.

"Mr Brown must have been saving it, especially for you."

"But why me? I do like the feel of it, though. When I stroke the skin, I feel like ..." She frowned a little, troubled by her inability to articulate her feelings, then corrected her mum. "It wasn't Mr Brown mum; it was a Clown."

"That's nice, babe ..." Simone replied, still somewhat distracted. She unlocked the car, then opened the rear door for Sally to get in.

Back in the bedroom, Hope interrupted ...

"Hold it." She leaned forwards, her face a little screwed up in confusion. "What's an orballoon?"

"What?" Sally frowned, surprised by the question.

"You called the balloon the clown gave you an orballoon. Where did that name come from?"

Looking slightly uncertain she replied vaguely. "Um, I think it's what the clown called it."

"Oh, right." Hope exchanged a furtive glance with Hannah. Whose eyes mirrored her friend's curiosity.

"I don't know. Maybe because it is shaped like a perfectly round orb. Anyway, shall I go on?" She shifted her position on the bed to get more comfortable.

She held the balloon tightly during the short drive home from the party, liking how it expanded around her fingers within the circle of her arms, and the soft feel of its surface against her cheeks when it bobbed against her face. She did not, however, like the stretchy, squelchy sounds her fingers made as she slowly drew them gently across the surface. It made her cringe. She appeared enchanted as she stared at the cheeky boy's face. Did he just wink at her? His eyes, fully open now, began to glow, and then they changed from regular pupils to spirals, turning around and around, reducing themselves to a point in the centre where the boy's pupils should have been. Glancing at her briefly in the rear-view mirror, Simone thought she was quieter than usual.

"Are you alright, Sal?" It was not like her not to be gushing and rehashing every moment of the party.

"Um, uh-huh ..." her response was low, calm, and did not seem out of the ordinary, quiet, or not.

"Good. Once we get home, tie the balloon somewhere in your room, alright? Somewhere safely out of reach of Serenity's sharp claws."

Though she nodded in agreement, saying, "Yeah. Her claws would burst it." Her eyes were fixed on the eyes of the boy on the balloon. "It can be tied to the topmost knob on my chest of drawers near the window." She suggested, "Then it'll be the first thing I see when I wake up and the last thing I see before I go to sleep."

"Yeah, that's a good place to tie it. An excellent suggestion. Almost home now, love." Simone looked thoughtful, her mind still on the earlier topic of conversation.

While the schoolchildren had been enjoying the party, the adults had been discussing the matter that began to worry her more, the more she heard people talking about it. She had thought this new virus was too far away to affect them in England. Except now, it was February, and this virus, called the coronavirus or covid 19, had spread to Italy, other European countries, the US, India, South America, and other areas. Some were treating it as serious. But the news could be making more or less of it as usual, sensationalising the story. Was it simply another form of bird flu and, to all accounts, relatively harmless?

Unfortunately, it was entirely a wait-and-see situation until trustworthy statements were forthcoming from a reputable source. She would speak with Richard about it. He would be home from the university by now. It was a conversation they could have once Sally had gone to bed.

3

Back in the bedroom ...

"Then what?" Hope prompted, chewing on another piece of toast.

"Well, I remember the ride home. I was thinking enviously of how lucky you two are to have such definite ambitions again."

While her friends stood out in their respective fields and had firm plans for their futures, she could not figure out what she wanted to do or where she wanted to go in terms of her life. She needed to figure out where her best talents lay and learn not to dither so much when faced with a choice. She was reasonably capable of most things. Alright at sports like netball and gymnastics, rubbish at arts and crafts admittedly, but great at communicating, interacting, and talking with people, or so she had been told. Intelligent, spontaneous, with an overly curious nature, she was good at figuring things out. Unfortunately, she had not yet discovered the value of being good at this or that being able to do so was quite a good skill. What good were they if she did not know how to use them? Her interests seemed to flit from one thing to another. Why was her future so unclear?

For someone so young, Sally had a natural talent that allowed her to look at a situation from more than just her perspective. Quick-witted and intuitive, she acted on what she felt was the right thing to do in most cases, regardless of who or what was being challenged or decided. Confident and friendly, she was well-liked among her peers as well as by the parents of her peers. She always had direct, intelligent questions for them, showing genuine interest, and would listen carefully to their answers. Details and information she subconsciously filed away to be used or shared on some other day in the future.

As a Libra, the sign represented by a set of scales in the zodiac, she was good at assessing a situation from both sides. Librans looked for balance in all things while attempting to keep everyone happy, or so her book, Astrology for your Astro Child, said. She sought to find a balance, whether involved in an argument, a discussion, or a debate. Or *be* the element of balance—the linchpin. She could turn her hand and mind to most things, saw the bigger picture well, and was interested in many topics beyond the usual range of ordinary childhood interests. For example, she was curious to know how things survived in nature, how animals were cared for by people, what made people act the way they did, and why foreign countries and cultures were so different from her own country and culture. She was a master of puzzles, crosswords, and board games like snakes and ladders, backgammon, and, more recently, chess. She also enjoyed the usual teen stuff like new tech, music, and fashion, and had joined the school drama club, having taken an interest in acting. But what would she do with all of this ... stuff? She wondered, frustrated. She recalled a conversation with her mum and dad about her future.

"It's normal not to have a clear path at your age, Sally." They had assured her on said occasion.

"As mature as you three are ..." Her dad began.

"Yeah, right, like thirteen-year-olds going on thirty." Simone joked.

Richard continued. "You're only thirteen. There is plenty of time to think about your future. I admit your friends are exceptionally talented in their respective fields, but you seem more of a people person."

"Yes, love. You make friends easily and can turn your hand reasonably well to anything." Her mum added encouragingly.

"But my friends have serious ambitions to achieve something specific, while I just dither ..."

"Yes, that is true of your friends," her dad interrupted. "But give yourself some credit. And I'm not simply saying this because I'm your dad and love you, either." He said, giving her a measured look. "On the one hand, it's good to know what you want to be and follow that dream enthusiastically and confidently. But the downside of having such a clear ambition so young is that those interests are all they know and all they focus on." She nodded a little as she listened.

"Your friends are very talented in their chosen fields, but you're talented in other ways. For example, you have a good, kind heart. You stand up for your friends, and having observed the three of you together, you are the one linking the other two. Would they even be friends if you were not there in the middle, making connections and finding ways to link your interests?" Sitting at the table eating their tea, she considered his words. "You've saved them from only focusing on one thing and possibly missing out on too much of all that should be enjoyed while you're still young." He continued. "You're gifted in bringing people together, initiating interesting conversations, and taking the time to consider situations from the point of view of others and your own perspective. Those are all good skills. Believe it or not, some people have no idea how to interact comfortably or break the ice with strangers. Not many in your age group, and even some adults, can see the world from another's perspective or start a conversation with whomever they meet without struggling." She was sitting with her chin resting in her hand and her elbows on the table now. "Listen, when you get older, you will have a world of options before you. These skills might not be leading you anywhere at your current age, but later, they will open doors to many paths for you to pursue. You can choose from many exciting fields of work to go into or start your own business," he encouraged.

"He's right, babe," Simone agreed. "You haven't found your niche yet, but in time you will. Your friends don't have such wide options when you think about it."

"Hmm, yeah, maybe," she agreed reluctantly, still a little unsure. "I suppose when you look at it that way, I do have a lot going for me."

"Rather ..." Richard agreed.

Her parents were correct in their assessment of the trio of girls' friendship and her unifying position. As her friends were so obsessed with their ambitions, she was the one who planned their non-sporty, non-arty leisure activities. She knew that if left to their own devices, Hannah would be holed up in her loft painting all day, and Hope would be off training somewhere. Although her interests were many and quite diverse, she was the most bookish and studious of the three girls and had a great memory. For a girl of her age, she understood quite a lot about life and the way things worked in the adult world. Hannah and Hope joked about changing her nickname to Wiki, short for Wikipedia, when she grew out of chewing gum—a far more suitable name, relevant forever, just like Juggernaut and Smudge-face.

Back in the bedroom ...

Hannah asked. "Then what happened?" While chewing on the end of a pencil. She was doodling on her sketch pad. "You said something about a party?"

"Yeah. That night, I dreamed about the party."

"What, my party?" She pulled a second coloured pencil out from where she had shoved it into her hair just above her left ear and put the point to the page of her book.

"No. It was another party. A different kind of party. A special, um, leap year party, I think."

"And the clown you mentioned? There wasn't a clown at my party. Can you describe this other party?"

"Show her what you've drawn so far." Hope suggested. "It might jog her memory a bit."

Sally leaned over to look at the sketch pad. Whilst listening to her description, Hannah had drawn the clown from the party using thick coloured pencils, almost precisely as Sally had described him.

"That's spot-on, Smudge." She looked away for a moment, again thoughtful. "I remember seeing him at the party and ..."

"You mean, you imagined seeing him at the party." Hope corrected. "No one else saw him, so it must have been imagined. Although I can't see how ..."

"Tell us about the party." Hannah interrupted, giving Hope an impatient look, her pencil poised. "Was it as crazy as my party was?" Sally stood up and went over to stand in front of the window. Thoughtful for a moment, she stared out at the row of houses opposite which mirrored her own in build and design.

The party she spoke of was indeed unusual. Looking around curiously for a few moments, it took her a minute to notice it was late at night, that there were three times more children than at Hannah's party, and they all wore items that hid their faces. From what she could see, she did not recognise any of the children behind the masks, hoods, and variety of hats and make-up. She looked down at herself and grinned. She was beginning to like this dream. Magic had transformed her long-sleeved plain faux-leather catsuit into a robust, sleek, flexible suit, that really was an all-in-one. She touched the snug hood around the back of her neck beneath her bushy pony feeling its cat-like points sticking up. Long tassels at her back and front hung from a belt to her knees, and the legs of her suit were tucked into long brown boots of a stretchy rubber with a cushiony softness within. She liked the cool, sophisticated outfit.

Standing alone on the room's threshold, she wondered where the chaperones were. She could see the smart clown towering over all the children who seemed ...!? She struggled to find the right words to describe the scene before her.

Within the room, a racy, terribly awful metal-rock type of music was blaring out from numerous hidden speakers, and some of the children were dancing wildly to it. To one side of the room, half a dozen youngsters were involved in a food fight while three or four others were spray painting the walls drawing faces, flowers, the sun, the moon, and other things. Others were running around spraying water pistols at everyone else, and the loud, continuous cries, shouts, screams, laughs, grunts, and lots of 'Oh's' exclaimed in sharp, high-pitched voices over the racket of bad taste music was painfully offensive to her sensitive nature. Try as she might, she could not grasp what anyone was saying, as no proper words were being spoken, only shouts, bellows, and laughter by everyone all at once.

"Where are the adults who should be watching everyone?" She mused out loud.

"Hello there, Sally." Said a loud, cheery voice from directly beside her. "You're late! But welcome to our Day Before Leap Year Day party!"

She turned to stare at the boy at her side, recognising him instantly.

"Hello. Welcome to your what? Leap year ...!? Um, aren't you the cheeky-looking boy on my orballoon?"

"Cheeky looking?" he asked looking perplexed. "If you say so, then yes, that's right. Very, very correct! I am so glad you recognised me. My name is Saxon."

"Saxon? Hello Saxon," she shook his outstretched hand.

"Do you know you are here by special, special invite?" He asked, then continued before she could answer. "We've been waiting for you for a long time, Sally. It's been four long, long years since the last leap year."

"You've been waiting for me? But why?" She jerked around and cringed suddenly as an ear-piercing scream rang out above all the other chaotic sounds.

"This is going to be such a fun, fun party Sally!" He gestured around them, indicating everything. "There's ice cream and cakes, games and toys, and many other children to play with."

"Just who are these kids? I mean, I don't recognise any of them from Hannah's party. Do you actually know them all?" She was looking around suspiciously. "And I don't play with toys," she added.

"No, of course you don't, silly me and yes, I do. I do! Every single one. We are all friends here to have fun. Come on, Sally, let's go and play. It's a leap year!" he sang gaily, his happy disposition becoming infectious.

"Alright." She agreed, swept up by his enthusiasm.

She followed the cheeky-looking boy as he led her through the large, spacious room, dodging past the other kids who continued to dance and play, past a long table piled high with platters of mostly her favourite foods: sausage rolls, samosas, crispy chicken strips and bowls of crisps, nuts, and pretzels. French sticks with a selection of fillers, jugs of juice, and large bottles of Coke and lemonade, filled the table. A large, chocolate-orange cake with thick icing rested in the centre of the table, with thirteen unlit candles standing tall on top. All set up on a pretty, plastic wipe clean tablecloth covering the table. Splashes of dripping liquid and bits of food were stuck to the wall beyond the table, made during the food fight.

"What shall we play?" She asked, stepping carefully around the chunks of food strewn all over the floor.

"I'll show you. We have a special leap year game we expect you to play! It is challenging but fun too. Then you can stay, stay in the party house forever! If you finish the game correctly," he grinned, nudging her in the ribs with an elbow.

"We?" she looked around. "Do you mean you and the clown? What do you mean by staying here forever? I don't want to stay here forever! Not with that dreadful music playing, and what is this game that can be finished correctly or incorrectly? What if I can't finish it at all?" she asked as they moved through the room.

"Such a smart, smart girl. A clever girl like you, of course, you will," he said confidently, intentionally sidestepping her questions. "It's one of your favourite games too. Come on, you will enjoy it, I promise!" He insisted, leading her over to a large, egg-shaped hole in the wall. A narrow ladder with six steps led up to the opening.

"What's this then? Where does it go? How do I play?" she asked curiously.

"Questions, questions, so many questions, when there's no need. Just grab onto the ladder there," he pointed, "climb up and go through the opening." He pointed again. "Follow the lighted feet through the curtains straight ahead of you. It is now two minutes to midnight, and you have a certain number of hours to reach the final ..." He stopped talking. Sally had hesitated behind him. She felt a bit mistrustful of Saxon; he seemed to be rushing her. For all his smiling and jolly, playful manner, there was something decidedly ominous about him.

Ominous. A word she had used in the proper context for the first time. She had picked a few words out of the dictionary during the word game she regularly played with her dad in which she had to use them in their proper context. Ominous was one of them.

Crossing her arms firmly, she stood on tip-toe to look through the opening. It was dimly lit inside. The only light she saw came from from a giant clock face directly in front of the opening. She glanced back into the room behind her. The other kids continued to play noisily, chasing each other around, eating and dancing with each other as though nothing were out of order. This was reassuring. He was looking at her questioningly now because she was dithering.

He is sly ...

The whispered warning flowed into her mind, the formed

letters floating and weaving across her inner vision.

He is devious. Do not trust him ...

Then she felt a slight tugging sensation on her wrist and glanced down at it. A loop of string was tied around it. She felt the tugging again and turned to see where the taut string ended. It stretched right across to the other side of the room and was attached to the hand of the big-faced fellow from her balloon. He was standing near the door, waving a hand at her. She grinned and waved back. The balloon string grew tighter as she did so.

"It's my orballoon, Saxon. He has my orballoon! Can I bring it with me? I must get it from him. He seems to be ... calling me." Unable to look away from the big-faced fellow, she felt a pleasant warmth emanating from his direction as a command unexpectedly popped into her head.

"Come to me, Sally, at once!" In the same voice that had whispered the warnings to her. A voice she knew she could trust. Winding the string around her fingers, she knew she had to go to him, at once. She turned away from the egg-shaped hole in the wall completely now as across the room, the big-faced fellow encouraged her on towards him. Smiling widely, he exaggeratedly mimed pulling her over to him in the way sailors pull in their ropes on a ship, working their hands over each other. She did not notice the other children automatically drifting out of her way as she moved through them. Her gaze was fixed trance-like upon the big-faced fellow. Saxon sighed in resignation. His smile faded, and he mumbled in a cross, frustrated tone.

"Brother! How irritating. I almost, *almost* had this one! One more minute and she would have been within the frame when the clock struck twelve, announcing the arrival of the leap year, twenty-four hours." His lips pressed together in a tight line. "She would have begun the long game, which is far more enjoyable, but now you will prepare her for the short game instead. Better than nothing, I suppose." Somewhat half-heartedly, his expression grim, he called, "Sally, come back!" His shout went unheard. "As always, once Noxas catches their eye, they are his until he lets them go. Unfortunately, the game will not begin on this night, but I will see you tomorrow, then maybe you'll stay with us forever." He muttered. He was turning away from the egg-shaped hole when his brother communicated with him telepathically; his cautious, warning tone stopping him in his tracks.

"That will not be so, brother. In your rushed efforts to get her involved in the game, you have yet to realise who we have here. Look again. Feel her energy."

A long silence ensued, while Saxon begrudgingly did so. Then he exclaimed, "Empress Salliniquai of the True Malsimily! How can that be?" He sent back telepathically, a note of excitement and deep respect reflected in his tone.

"Somehow, it seems fitting. Considering it is our last opportunity to save and protect those chosen to lead during the new Aquarian age."

"Yes, very fitting. Perhaps this is also why she keeps referring to the balloon the clown gave her as an orballoon."

"The orb shape must have jogged her Empresserial memory of her own orb, somehow."

"Quite possible, yes. If so, then all is happening according to the Divine plan. The rules of the previous games may be a bit different from this one. We must watch out for this. There is a reason she is here now on the cusp of our final leap year, right before the Great Suffering sweeps across the physical human realm. That reason, as always, must be for the good of the whole."

Noxas nodded slowly, "I agree, brother. But how is it she cannot remember herself as herself? That is unusual, is it not?"

Saxon shrugged. "Hmm, perhaps. Although a lot older and far wiser than us all, she has incarnated within the body of a young girl. Perhaps this is why."

"So then, Sally will play the short game on this occasion."

"That is a given. To be honoured by the energy of the Empress, this can be no incidental accident brother."

"Agreed. The time of Great Suffering is close now. It's a shame that many people's creative dreams, ambitions, hopes and whatnot will soon end due to this dreadful contagion."

"Many hopes will be dashed as the world faces a threat that will change, delay or end the paths of millions of people worldwide." Saxon thought with grim finality. "Brother, I feel quite depressed. I think I will cheer myself up by trying some of that chocolate-orange cake." Turning abruptly, he headed towards the table piled high with party food.

Meanwhile, in a somewhat hypnotic daze, Sally wound the string in loops around her hand as she followed it to its end. The closer she got to the big-faced fellow, the harder it was to see him. He seemed to be slowly fading. When she was just a few steps away, a trio of boys noisily crossed her path, and she had to stop short, or they would have barrelled straight into her. When she looked to where the big-faced fellow had been waiting for her, all that remained was her balloon, floating gently, attached to the string wrapped around her wrist. She reached out towards it, and in that instant, everything around her vanished as a huge puff of smoke appeared around her. She was suddenly as light as a feather, floating around in a strange magical energy field.

"Wow, where am I?" She gasped in awe. "Am I *inside* my orballoon?"

"Oh, come now, Sally, you know exactly where you are! You just do not believe it. Even in your dreams, the sensation is not new to you." A gentle, soothing voice responded. Saxon shot him a warning thought. *"Careful, brother, careful."*

"Where are you? Why are you hiding?" She asked, glancing around the smoky enclosure. "How can I be inside my orballoon?" She heard a deep, rolling chuckle as the big-faced fellow's head materialised beside her, huge and dramatic.

"You see. You are twice as smart as we imagined!" He said, with a happy, satisfied look. He introduced himself. "I am Noxas. I am to prepare you for the short Leap Year game challenge. It is one I know you can win as proof of ..."

"Careful, brother, careful."

"So, this is a dream?" she interrupted. "I'm dreaming?!" she grinned. "This is a very odd dream, Noxas," she was now upside down in the purple and silver haze.

"Aren't they all? However, let us not think about that for the moment. I had to get your attention before you went through the Egg-trance. You have much to commit to memory on this night before the Leap year day begins tomorrow."

"Egg-trance? What's an Egg-trance?" She was trying to see his eyes but could not whilst she kept floating about.

"The Egg-trance is the doorway to the Leap Year game, the game you will play."

"Oh, I see," she nodded thoughtfully. Though she had not heard these terms before, she somehow understood the meaning.

"Let's not think about that either for the moment. Just know that I believe in you. I know you can do this!" His huge lips curved upwards beneath the rim of his hat. "Parties are so much fun, aren't they? Lots of fun and games." He chuckled again.

"Yeah, they are," she agreed. "But what's this special game I'm to play? Will I like playing it? I hope it's not some silly old game for little kids."

"Oh yes, it is one you're quite lucky at playing. The Game of ..." he paused. A low, decidedly mysterious-sounding chuckle rumbled in his throat. "You will see tomorrow. The game begins tomorrow."

"What *is* The Game? Tell me what it is, or I'm not playing!" she demanded crossly. Her brow wrinkled in a stubborn frown, her lips pursed defiantly, and she crossed her arms in front of her chest. While floating upside down, however, her defiance was amusing to Noxas. He chuckled, shaking his head from side to side.

"Hmm ... unfortunately for you, but fortunately for us, it is far too late for that sort of empty threat, Empress ..." His voice took on an authoritative tone. "I am here to make sure all that happens happens fair and square as it happens. Still, that's the spirit, young Sally! The kind of spirit needed to win this highly hazardous, dangerous game."

"Dangerous? Erm, hang on a minute. Empress?" She was growing confused with his double talk. "Why did you call me Empress?"

"Challenging, I mean, not dangerous, no, and I said to *Impress*," he lied quickly, lowering his head so the rim of his hat covered his entire face. *I must be careful. She has no awareness of her true self in this realm.* "The Clown chose you to play, and no one can stop the process once it has begun. So, you will play tomorrow."

"You haven't told me what the game is, what the stakes are or anything. How can I prepare to play a game I don't know and have no reason to play? I mean, what happens when I win?" Noxas smiled inwardly at her confident assumption of winning the game. His grin broadened under the hat's rim.

"If you win, you get to stay with us, under our protection and no longer part of the world, until ..."

She interrupted. "You mean," she hesitated. "You mean I'd never see my family or friends again?"

"You will see them again but not until ... until it's safe to do so ..." *And if they survive.*

Safe? She was beginning to regret her initial excited curiosity about playing a game through interactive dreaming. Could what Noxas be saying be true? Not seeing family and friends again was no reward for winning a game in her book. They might change their minds and choose someone else to play if she acted up somehow.

"And if I lose?" She asked, hoping it would mean she was released from the game but mentally preparing herself for the worst anyway. His response was blunt and to the point.

"If you lose. You perish."

"Perish?" She swallowed deeply, holding his gaze steadily. "Die, you mean?" She scoffed dismissively. "How can I die when this is all just a dream?"

"How indeed?" he murmured, somewhat enigmatically. He shrugged off her curiosity almost carelessly. "Don't dwell on that aspect of the game. Nothing is set in stone, especially not for you, Empress." He saw her look and quickly continued. "I mean, I digress."

She frowned suspiciously, thinking that his responses were decidedly enigmatic and carefully measured. She wasn't stupid. This was the third time he had referred to her as Empress. The clown and referred to her as Empress too, then both pretended they hadn't. There was more to this than meets the eye. What was really going on? Inwardly, she chalked up using the word enigmatic in its proper context. She remembered something the clown had said and asked,

"Why me anyway? Why was I chosen for this ... honour? There were plenty of others at Hannah's party, so why choose me?"

Noxas's giant head cocked to one side. "I believe you met certain special criteria. But that is a question for the clown. Maybe you will get to ask it later if you play. Besides, things are already set in motion, and there is no ... going ... back." He accentuated these last words in a tone that was final, and a steely no-nonsense look had entered his eyes.

"Isn't it unfair that I lose my life, whether I win or lose. Why should I even bother to play?"

"You should bother because one cannot un-bake a cake once the mix is in the oven." Though she could not see his eyes past his hat's wide, low brim, she sensed him watching her closely. "The outcome is not necessarily set. There is another strong, spiritually important element to this I do not have time to explain. For now, you must not let anything distract you from doing your best to win, regardless of what is gained at the end of it. The important thing to know is your performance in the game will determine the outcome. It is not simply about winning or losing." His voice was confident and persuasive.

"No, really?" She snapped sarcastically, regretting getting mixed up in this. What started as a surprising bit of fun now felt like she was doomed, whichever way it turned out. She was being set up to fail so they could keep her with them. She could think of nothing worse than being trapped at that party with those unruly, wild children forever or even for five minutes. Unfortunately, it appeared she had no choice but to play. Once in the game, she could find another way to return to the real world. She took a deep breath and, drawing herself together, said, "Alright. I'm in. What do I have to do?"

Having watched her facial expressions as she worked out her options, Noxas nodded approvingly, leaned in closer and spoke softly.

"Now, listen to me carefully. It is vitally important that you do exactly as I say." She leaned towards him. "Concentrate on my voice. You have important things to remember ..." Her eyelids drooped as she held steady within the balloon, and her facial features smoothed out, becoming relaxed and serene. "There are three things you must bring from your world into ours. You must remember exactly what to do with them because you will be alone tomorrow night. You must complete the game before the stroke of midnight on Leap Year Day, and I can only help you at the end, at the time of the final leap. Now, listen carefully, and *remember* ..."

4

Saturday 29th February. Leap year day ...

The day dawned bright and clear with the mild temperatures continuing as the forecasters predicted. As the sun rose above the eastern horizon it struggled to shine its light through the grey sky scattered with drifting clouds.

In her untidy, predominantly purple bedroom, Sally woke up with no memory of the dream from the night before. Glancing up at the balloon floating above her dressing table beside the window reminded her of party the night before and she suddenly remembered all the exciting things she would be doing that day. Thinking of those activities, she leapt out of bed and headed to the bathroom to get ready.

Back in the bedroom ...

"Things get a bit fuzzy here. What did we do that day?" she asked, turning from the window to look back at her friends. Hope had gone over to her dressing table, picked up a small brush and returned to the bed, where she began combing it briskly through her pony tail to smooth out a knot. Sally laughed.

"For God's sake, that's the karm's brush. Use this one." She picked up a larger, human-sized brush from the dresser and threw it to her. Hannah chuckled softly; head bent low over her pad.

Catching the hairbrush, Hope sat more comfortably, then looked up and said,

"Does the job just as well." She hesitated. "The karms brush? What's a karm?"

"Cat, it's the cat's brush, I said."

"Nooo, you said it was a ..."

"Oh damn!" Hannah suddenly exclaimed, then said apologetically, "Sal, I've dropped my juice, sorry. Can you get a cloth or something?"

"Oh god, it's all over the rug," Sally cried, leaping up and rushing out to get a cloth from the bathroom. As soon as she left the room, Hannah turned to Hope and whispered.

"Hope, stop challenging what she says for now. We have to get to the bottom of everything about the weekend before she forgets it all. We can ask about her funny references later. Alright?"

Hope stared at her, a puzzled expression in her eyes. "But I only asked about ..."

"*Alright?!*" Hannah whispered again, firmly.

"Alright, *alright* ..." Hope threw up her hands. "I don't see what the big deal is, but okay."

In the telling of her tale, Sally has begun to cross-reference details from the three realms of nature, meaning the energy of the Empress is close to being fully infused with her own. During her trial and for the rest of her life, she will be affected by the Hereditary Kee of the Malsimily.

When she used the term karm instead of cat, she was referring to a creature found in the Land of Ludonia - the realm of the subconscious, in the Realm of the Empress, on the Planes of the Malsimily, and of course, within the human physical realm, for the two are one and the same.

***

A note from the Timekeeper ... the origins of the Malsimily, the Empress, and the charge of the Narrator...

The Malsimily, in its entirety, relates to a great people, a place of unimaginable magical wonder, a triple-layered language, and several other fascinating things within the spiritual realm. Since the beginning of time, the eternal beings of the Malsimily have carried out essential functions to strengthen spiritual integrity throughout the known human universe. These mystical beings have influenced the Earth's progress on many occasions to prevent it from spiralling down the plug hole of spiritual destruction.

For the Malsimily, time is not as humans understand it, but time as it exists in the spiritual realms – a vast, eternal blanket of time in which we are one of the nine Timekeepers. Part of our charge is to watch over and guide all seeded beings, the Empress in this case, supported by the Knightly Legends and three other teachers. As a seed of the True Malsimily, the Empress Salliniquai has a soul at peace with itself and in her realm, she is Mother Nature, the

Goddess of Gaia, and the Empress of all.

The Malsimily, in their superior wisdom, sent the Empress Salliniquai, a being of the purest good blessed with a unique imagination, formidable magical powers and exceptional creative abilities, to balance the spiritual essence of the three realms of nature. A charge of the highest order, her arrival and governance would ensure the protection and spiritual eternity of all living souls in the Realm of the Empress, the human physical realm known as Earth, and in the subconscious realm of Ludonia.

Her charge was three-fold. First, she was to evolve her nature within her self-created realm in preparation for completing a challenging journey across her magical lands. Second, after making said journey, she was to sacrifice herself to the Distance realm, and third, she must challenge the emperor for the right to usher in the Aquarian age on the Planes of the Malsimily.

We are translating this epic journey because no human can understand Malsimily in its designation as a complicated, triple-layered language and if truth be told, at the start of this translation, we were far too busy watching, waiting, and ensuring the paths of time ran true to become involved in all the pesky little dramas humans tend to get themselves embroiled in. However, quite unexpectedly, during our lengthy observations, we have grown fond of the Earth's people (not our usual behaviour).

The human potential to nurture and love all people is so great we could not resist becoming a bit intrigued. Later, as time went on and we observed the people further, we became fascinated and absolutely hooked. Due to our thought-amplifying, mind-reading power, we know the thoughts of all beings within the Realm of the Empress, and all whose energy signature originates from there, which includes the knights of the Brotherhood of the Nine and the empresserial hosts.

Our omnipresent, umbrellica-soy magic is more potent in the human physical realm and extends to all humans. We can therefore, focus on those connected to our charges in bonds of love and friendship, those viewed as enemies, anyone involved in the creation of the Great Suffering, all who ... well, it is easier to say almost everyone, really. However, we shall only translate those thoughts pertinent to Empress Salliniquai's story.

In humans, we saw hopes and dreams that reached for the stars in refreshing innocence. Millions respect all forms of life, and an untold number treat their fellow men and women with compassion, tolerance, and kindness. Many open-minded individuals are attuned to the true nature of the world and the true purpose of life; in fact, we now feel blessed to have observed the true face of humankind.

***

Back in the bedroom ...

Hope confirmed her agreement again just as Sally returned with a large wet cloth and immediately began to dab the rug with it.

"Here, let me do it. I spilt it." Hannah insisted, taking it from her. "Go on with the story."

"Ok, thanks. Where were we? What did we do?" She moved over to the bed and sat down again.

"Well, um ... let's see. We spent part of the day swimming at the Dome, which was totally radical. Maybe you got bruised in there?" Hope suggested. The Dome was a huge water park a short bus ride away, with pools, slides, tunnels, fountains, and waterfalls.

"After swimming, we went to the mall," Hannah added, flipping a page of her sketch pad over so she had a clear sheet in front of her again.

The girls had spent most of the day hanging around various eateries, such as Ice-cream Dream, Rumbles Rolls and Henderson's Hamburgers. Later, they had gone to the cinema, along with half of the girls and boys from the two local schools. Lots of popcorn got thrown around, and while the older boys teased one another and larged it up, the older girls tried to act as cool as the Kardashians.

"Yeah, that's right. I remember being at the mall and ... did we go to the cinema as well?"

"We did. You sat in the back row with Roy Jenkins." Hope said a bit too causally.

"What! I never did. Did I?" She exclaimed—a distasteful look on her face. Roy Jenkins was a big show off all the cool girls fancied. She frowned an intense stare at Hannah, searching for confirmation.

"Don't Hope," Hannah said reproachfully. "Ignore her; she's pulling your leg. He is such an idiot. You know we all think so."

"Hmm ..." Sally mumbled, giving Hope, whose face was a mask of innocence, an unimpressed look. "Once or twice during the day, I got a funny feeling which made me anxious. It felt like something strange was about to happen, and I had to prepare for it. An important challenge of some sort." She could not explain the feeling then or now. Not in words. She only knew that some event was drawing near, involving something she was supposed to do during the night. Something had nagged at the back of her mind throughout the day, but as she was enjoying herself with her friends, the thoughts faded away, staying just out of reach until night approached.

"Hmm, the plot thickens ..." murmured Hope, bunching and rubbing her hands together as she hunched her shoulders. When Hannah sent her a warning look, she pretended not to see.

That Saturday night, in the darkness of her bedroom, her night light, as usual, threw projections of the zodiac signs across her walls and ceiling. She recited all the zodiac signs like a lullaby, which always helped her fall asleep. Serenity, lying stretched out at the bottom of her bed, was fast asleep. Her ginger and white furry tummy moved up and down with each breath while her whiskers twitched sporadically.

Abruptly, she sat up and turned to stare at the face of Saxon, the boy on the balloon. His strange eyes began to twirl and spin in spirals again, drawing her in. In a hypnotic trance, she got off the bed, retrieved her school bag and removed her pencil case. Opening the case, she pulled out three extra thick, coloured pencils. Laying these on the bed, she took the empty goodie bag from where it hung over the back of her desk chair, and laid it down beside the pencils. Hooking her fingers gently beneath Serenity's collar, she fumbled with the catch, released it, and placed it beside the other items.

She looked towards the balloon again. Saxon's face smiled down at her as it bobbed from side to side, then as the balloon turned, the half-covered face of Noxas, his lips wide beneath the rim of his hat, smiled down at her too. For nine long minutes, she stared at the balloon transfixed.

A remembered instruction then entered her mind, and she scooped the items up and threw them directly at the turning face of Noxas, stretched over the silvery purple skin of the balloon. Miraculously, the objects disappeared into the skin.

A lightening bright flash of light cast sharp shadows across the room. A gust of wind, strong enough to blow her back a step, whipped around her for a few seconds, its origins unknown.

Moments later, all was calm again. She blinked three times quickly, then, still in a daze, returned to her bed and slipped beneath the duvet again. Serenity, unaffected by the short, compact tornado, lay undisturbed. Her whiskers twitched a little, but other than that, she appeared unaffected by the windy, bright conditions in the room a moment before. In less than a minute, she was fast asleep and again, she dreamed ...

Back in the bedroom ...

Hope sat forwards and rubbed her hands together again.

"Right. Now we are getting to the juicy bit. This game you had to play."

Hannah had drawn a rough sketch of Sally in bed with a circle of astrological signs floating above her head.

"Keep the descriptions coming," she said. "I'll have your mysterious story in pictures by the time you finish, in case you forget again."

Sally sighed gratefully. "Excellacious. Thanks, Smudge." At the strange reference, Hope looked at Hannah curiously while Hannah gazed back at her with a mild, warning look, urging her not to say anything in her unspoken communication.

Back at the party, Sally now stood before the egg trance. Her hands grasped the second to the top rung of the ladder, and she was about to pull herself up and through it. The clamour she could hear from the other children enjoying themselves was louder than the music. She was almost glad to be going into the egg-trance, if only to get away from the dreadful racket some idiots on the planet called music. She had tied the string from her balloon securely around her right thumb. The length of which kept the balloon floating a dozen inches above her hand. Within those inches, three items, encased in individual, mini-transparent bags and reduced in size, were attached to the string like charms on a chain. Serenity's cat collar, the goodie bag from the party, and the three pencils banded together.

"Well, here goes," she murmured lightly, squaring her shoulders purposefully.

With a gymnast's flexible grace, she manoeuvred herself through the egg trance, then jumped down on the other side of the opening. The moment her feet touched the ground, the noise from the party cut off into silence behind her. She looked back, but the egg-shaped opening was no longer there. The large clock face she had seen briefly the night before hung in its place. The time was 9.02 pm.

Along the narrow corridor to her right, a dark gloom stretched away. To her left, the hall led towards a subdued brightness not too far away, with several feet-shaped spotlights leading the way. She felt a slight tugging sensation and understood she was being drawn along by an invisible force towards a pair of heavy, floor to ceiling, dark purple curtains a few dozen feet ahead of her. With a sense of youthful daring and an almost casual acceptance of her fate, she surrendered to the unusual energy flow and walked down the corridor, placing her feet on the lighted footsteps. She was *really* there, she thought. Really in a magical place about to play Saxon and Noxas's leap year game of ... the leap year game of ... oh, whatever he called it. It was no longer important. Thinking this made her more determined to win and she quickened her pace.

For a moment, she thought back to Hannah's dinner party when she had been stuffing her face with pizza. At the time, they couldn't stop talking about their plans for the rest of the weekend. Then she thought of her first dream of the strange party, where everyone wore masks, ran around throwing food, and was writing and drawing on the walls. She was excited and totally up for playing this magical leap-year game. As her mum often said, stranger things have happened.

This was not the first strange thing to happen to her, and she could almost normalise it, especially as it was just a dream. But was it? Again, a sense of there being much more to this game than meets the eye, had her on high alert.

When she reached the curtains, they swept apart slowly, but quite dramatically. Then she stepped through into the huge, dark space beyond. She could not tell if she were inside or outside because it was so vast and gloomy with a light breeze of relatively fresh air. She gasped in amazement at the sight before her, then grinned incredulously, her features reflecting wonder as glittering light shone down on her upturned face. She was looking at the most unbelievable sight she had ever seen and was completely overwhelmed by its garish, totally over-the-top, glittery brightness.

The shadowy, dark cavernous space before her was illuminated by a matrix of brightly lit squares at its centre. Upon the squares was a giant, three-story high, three-dimensional Snakes and Ladders game, structured like a cube.

"Oh my gosh! Oh wow! Oh, Saxon, you were right." She gasped. "This isn't just another board game. This is something special and real! Well, as real as a dream can be, I suppose." Her wide-eyed stare took in the numbered squares with sparkling corners and ladders, some of which looked suspiciously plain against the bright background of the rest of the enormous structure. The lowest row of squares was dark and hard to see through. Within its smoky, swirling mists, she saw oddly angled staircases that curved and twisted away into a shadowy, green-tinged gloom, leading off and up into other squares. The drifting mists thickened and then thinned again, showing her different ladders in higher squares. These were long and metal, short and wide, and wooden or made of rope. With a sinking feeling of dread, she reasoned that where there were real ladders, there would be real snakes, too—snakes suspiciously missing from the three-dimensional structure before her. She thought she saw the shadow of a colossal snake weaving from side to side in an evil way in the background; then it was gone. Had she been mistaken? A trick of the light, perhaps?

Several squares had strange, snake-skin decorated sides, which made her wonder about their effect on the game. She was excited rather than daunted by the sight of the game however, for this was all simply a dream. She could face anything dressed in her 'Cat Woman' outfit, a vital factor of the dream as it would allow her to climb, manoeuvre, run and jump in relative comfort and ease. She was unafraid of the intimidating structure before her because the board's design was familiar.

"This is awesome," she said coolly to herself. She felt a sudden rush of heat along the length of her right arm as the balloon string pulled taut for a moment. With a sharp, ripping sound, the transparent bag holding the goody bag detached from the string, and dropped to the floor, then slowly began to unfold itself. It had transformed into a map of the game, drawn on a large piece of soft, flexible parchment. Picking it up, she contemplated it for a moment, but it looked just like the board of a typical snakes and ladders game, with one difference. A small 'Cat Woman' figure, leaning against a giant pencil like a steadying staff, stood on the board before a line labelled 'START.' An arrow pointed away from the figure to the left, towards a curving, snake-skinned corridor, numbered square one in the game. Having stared long enough in wonderment at what was before her and down at the map board, despite her misgivings about the suspiciously absent snakes, she remained excited by the challenge of playing the game.

"Right, so. How do I begin?" She mused lightly, stepping forward and crossing the threshold from the corridor onto the board proper. The balloon floating at her side suddenly burst, and the pencils and cat collar fell to the floor as the torn pieces vanished into thin air. She gasped in surprise, then swallowed deeply, her hand on her chest to calm her skittish heartbeat. It was just the orballoon, you idiot. But ... was that meant to happen? And what is that she can hear?

From a direction she could not ascertain, a hollow, ticking sound had begun. Then she heard a snake's long, deep, dreadful hiss, along with the slithery, dragging, shifting sound of something bulky moving about. It echoed hollowly, seemingly coming from all directions. She swallowed deeply and glanced down at the floor where the items previously tied to the string lay. One of the miniaturised pencils had quadrupled in size, while the other two, along with the cat's collar, remained small. Scooping everything up, she examined the oversized pencil thoughtfully as she tucked the other two and the cat's collar inside a hidden pocket in the thigh of her outfit.

For a minute, she was unsure of what to do next. Then she looked to her left and noticed an archway with the word START burned into the wood and square one printed on the ground beneath it. Neither had been there before she looked away to retrieve her fallen items.

The entrance to the game was through the arch and down the corridor which she could see led directly into the huge structure in the centre of the space. She walked beneath the arch and for a few moments it remained dark, and then began to lighten.

The corridor was perfectly square-shaped, with the walls,

ground, and ceiling measuring the same on all sides. The floor was covered with a brownish-gooey substance, and a sharp, raw smell rose from it supplanting the fresh air she had been breathing seconds before. The snake skin pattern of a Burmese Python, coloured mostly in brown and yellow, with a little black, decorated the ceiling and walls. Having identified the snake the skin belonged to, her curiosity had her reaching out to stroke the wall. However, just before her fingers touched the surface, an angry hiss and a decidedly creepy ripple along the wall made her snatch her hand back. The wall had moved, but in a way that... no. That wasn't possible. The wall seemed to ... breathe like it was somehow ... alive! The walls did not just look like snakeskin; they would feel like snake skin too, she thought.

Having stroked a Burmese python once when it was hung around Hope's very brave neck during their class trip last year, she knew what the skin would feel like. At the time, while most of the other students had looked at the snakes for a few moments, then moved along to the next glass-walled enclosure, Hannah, Hope, and herself especially, with her interest in all creatures, particularly exotic ones, had taken the time to read all about the different species on display: Burmese pythons, milk snakes, and adders. Hope had been brave, while the rest of the class were chicken. Only when she promised it would not bite her if she stroked it did she do so, nowhere near its head, though.

In the corridor, while her concentration was elsewhere, she slipped over and just about managed not to fall flat on her face. She caught herself with both hands sinking wrist-deep in the goo. Her face twisted in disgust as she wiped her mucky hands on her legs. Paying proper attention now, she walked slowly and steadily, placing one foot carefully in front of the other, as though walking along a bench at gym club. The goo was growing steadily thicker and deeper, though, and when she wiped a sweaty hand across her face leaving a dark stain across her cheek and chin, she gave up trying to keep any part of herself clean. It was just her luck that the goo was everywhere. She hated being messy...

Continuing, she cringed back from the walls as the tunnel twisted and turned, sloping down and then up in places. The design of it made no logical sense to her, but she concluded that it was probably a normal type of passage for a snake. Sporadically, a gust of wind surged through the game, bringing the foul stench of what she assumed was the snake pit with it. Wrinkling her nose, she almost slipped over again and had to slow further to slog her way more carefully through the goo. She tried not to wonder what it was, and momentarily wondered at the possibility of her being *inside* a snake. But the idea seemed too uncomfortable and unthinkable to be true. She focused on putting one foot in front of the other again. Moving too quickly was risky. She did not want to fall over again.

The corridor was growing narrower and narrower. It was not until she was knee deep in goo, the walls were almost touching her shoulders and her face was streaked with grime that she remembered the hood of her catsuit. If she pulled it up it would stop the goo from getting in her hair. Quickly, she pulled the hood over her head, gasped, and then grinned. Instantly, in one smooth ripple, the suit had become a sort of wetsuit with just her eyes, nose and mouth exposed. Just in time and perfect for these conditions, she thought. The goo was almost waist high now.

Growing increasingly apprehensive, she kept going, knowing she could not turn back. The walls were close enough to touch her shoulders now, and she had to turn sideways to pass through. She forced herself to keep going, wondering why the map had given no clue about the corridor's actual type, length, or whether she was going to end up drowning in whatever this rising goo was. She tried hard not to think about it.

5

Back in her bedroom, she continued ...

"At the time, rather than dwell on the uncomfortably narrowing corridor and rising goo, I wondered what Hannah would make of it." She rearranged her position on the bed again. "I tried to imagine how your arty eyes would see it. You would have been fascinated with the snakeskin-designed walls. I remember thinking, if you could make your paintings look half as real as these walls, you'd be quids in one day." Hannah chuckled but did not look up from her drawing book.

Back in the game ...

Sally smiled at the thought of her friend, then focussed her attention back on the game. She had to squeeze between the breathing, snakeskin walls now. Knowing they were alive and with hissing echoing around her from all sides, she grew more tense and cringed as she squeezed through. And then, just when she thought the walls would squish her if she went any further, she reached a cross-section where the left and right off-shoots sloped downwards, and the gunk began to drain away. Rechecking the map, she continued straight ahead, finding the corridor widening again.

The cross-section she was looking for had seemed close on the map, and she was out of breath when she finally reached it. Stained and dirty, she paused to bend over, resting her hands on her thighs just above her knees for a minute as she looked around, almost convinced she had made a wrong turn, but no, there it was. A large, square, silvery die face, set low in the wall with its bottom edge almost touching the ground. Its mirrored surface shone clean and pure in its surround of the gently pulsing snake skin. She sighed with relief, pulled back her hood and stared curiously at her reflection momentarily fascinated by what the mirrored surface of the die face revealed. It was a series of brief impressions. The first was of a huge emerald green symbol of Venus, then of herself, in her catsuit, then of another young girl whose aura exuded a powerful energy, followed by images of several other, older women.

Some of Noxas's words of caution returned to her then, reminding her of the instructions and the warnings he had given her the night before. She smiled to herself reassuringly as the strange reflection disappeared and she saw the die face again clearly. She now understood how to play the game.

Stepping up to the die face, she considered it for a moment then looked down. The edges of the square on the ground beneath it lit up when she stepped onto it. As she pondered the shining, die face, the outline beneath her slowly faded away. The face on the wall was four times the size of the regular snakes and ladders board she had received on her eighth birthday, with three black holes instead of dots.

She folded the map and tucked it securely into another thigh pocket. Then, holding the pencil she had retrieved by the blunt end, she aimed it at the centre of one of the black dots, then pushed it firmly through. With a sharp, popping sound, the pencil and her hand went through the black up to her elbow. Instantly numbed, a tingling sensation she did not like began to creep up her arm. It took some effort, but after a few moments she managed to manipulate and then wrench her arm free. She stretched and curled her fingers for a moment to clear the numbness and looked at the pencil. Half of it had been sliced cleanly off.

A loud, booming clang coming from somewhere behind and below her was followed by the sound of a heavy chain being drawn across a hard surface, and the same slithery, dragging sound she had heard before. This time when the chilling gust of wind blew past, the foul, pungent, disgustingly sharp, mouldy smell, almost made her gag. Noxas had warned her about the giant snake lying in wait in its pit.

Crumbs. What a stench! Had she made a mistake and set the snake free?

"Oh damn, I think I poked the wrong hole. Noxas, I picked the wrong one! Maybe I'm not as smart as you thought after all." She muttered, then shouted, "What do you think?" No response. But was the master snake just a step closer to being freed, or was it free already? A sudden, hideously thick, guttural hiss echoed loudly all around her. It sounded so close she spun around fast with eyes wide and frightened, trying to look everywhere at once. A chilling finger of fear ran down her spine. She had thought the snake was right behind her.

Although the passage was empty, she wondered again whether the master snake had been set free by her wrong choice. The stench from the snake's pit, ten times worse than the smell already apparent, whooshed past again, filling her nostrils and lifting tendrils of her hair in the strong gust of air. Not wanting to overthink it or begin to dither, she turned and stabbed the now half pencil into one of the remaining two holes and holding her breath, she waited ... and waited, in what felt like the longest, most complete silence, in the history of long, complete silences, ever. Her eyes narrowed slightly when she heard the suspenseful, tell-tale sound of a mechanism winding into action. A moment later, something brushed against her left shoulder, startling her. A long rope ladder had dropped down from a trap door above. She sighed with relief as she grabbed it, mumbling,

"Obviously more scared than I thought. So, on my very first go, I made a mistake which probably released the snake. Silly, silly, *silly* karm," then with good humour. "Lucky for me, I have nine lives."

Dropping the half pencil into a side pocket, she gripped the ropy sides of the ladder and began to climb. Reaching the top, she manoeuvred her head and shoulders through the trap door opening, but as she leaned her waist on the edge and swung her legs up, the half pencil fell from her pocket. Pausing halfway through the trapdoor, she bit her lip as she watched it bounce and roll away along the corridor below. *Damn.* Should she go back for it? Before she could decide, she heard a distant, squelching, shifting sound that seemed to be getting louder. Whatever it was, and by it, she meant snake or snakes, were getting closer.

Hurriedly pulling herself up through the trap door, she glanced around briefly. She was in a narrow, dimly lit tunnel with moist, muddy brown walls and faded, uneven lines on the floor, marking out faint squares. Crouched in a pose like one she had seen one of her Cat Women do, she closed the trap door. She could see quite far along the tunnel in both directions, and though the approaching sounds were quite disturbing, she remained poised, alert, and ready for anything. She took a few seconds to listen more closely, trying to ascertain in which direction the sound was coming from.

Along the length of the tunnel, several single light bulbs with wide gaps between them hung in a straight line. Dropping down from the centre of the curved ceiling, they shed light upon the mud-stained walls and rays of dim, yellowish light glowed eerily beneath each bulb. She stared down the tunnel, squinted, and then turned her head so she could hear better. Soon enough, a huge, writhing shadow appeared, moving closer and closer to her. Her eyes widened in fear as she saw it was not just one snake. It looked like ... hundreds!

The heaving, squirming mass of milk snakes hurried towards her, their slick, slithering bodies a sickening mix of horror and disgust. Terrified and overwhelmed with fear, she froze. Still in her crouched position, she stared at the shadowy sight for a moment, and then a spine-tingling, itchy sensation under her skin jerked her out of her stunned state, compelling her to act for her own survival.

An insistent pressure against her thigh prompted her to take out Serenity's collar. In her hand it magically returned to its normal size again, prompting her to use it. At once, she knew what to do. She kept her eyes fixed on the approaching mass for a few dreadfully long seconds, with hands were shaking so much she could not connect the clasp. She backed away towards the wall and fastened it around her left leg just above the knee, hooked her right leg behind her, then sat cross-legged on the floor. Perhaps sensing they were about to be denied their feast, the snakes speeded up their efforts. The front runners of the swarm, were barely six feet away when an orb-shield, with a sparkling, greenish tint to it, suddenly appeared enclosing her inside. Beads of sweat stood out on her forehead as relief flooded through her. Her view beyond the orb was hazy through the thin membrane, and she hoped with all her heart, that it was strong enough to hold them off.

Back in her bedroom, she recounted to her friends ...

"In the nick of time, it formed an orb-shield around me. I felt completely safe inside it."

Head cocked to one side, her pencil poised, Hannah prompted, "Can you describe what it was like?"

"Um ... it was like ..." she paused, considering, "like being inside one of my bubble-gum bubbles, except when I pushed at the skin of the orb-shield it was really tough, but weirdly flexible too. I'd describe it as being as solid as a rock, the way it held the buggers off, but that contradicts what it actually was." *Contradicts; another word used correctly from our word-play game.*

Back in the game ...

Inside the orb-shield, she was safe. Although it was an utterly strange thing, it somehow, felt familiar. Her shaky breaths and wildly beating heart began to slow to a normal level as she tried to peer through the skin. When the snakes were almost on top of her,

her eyes opened so wide she thought they might pop out of their sockets. She scooted back within the orb-shield so that it leaned right up against the wall; then waited for her very up close and personal view of what was coming for her.

Out of the darkness, they came. Like a wave within a churning sea, their wiggling bodies almost filled the width of the tunnel as their dark, cold, lifeless eyes reflected the light from the overhead bulbs. In one great heaving mass of slimy, slithering bodies, hundreds of Milk snakes, their skin a patchwork of red, divided by black-edged white stripes, rushed towards her. She stared out at the sickening, creepy sight as the first of the wigglers slithered their way over the orb-shield, leaving gooey, crisscrossing trails over its impenetrable skin. Her stomach churned seeing their long, pale underbellies slithering over her.

Their numbers increased, and as the heavy thumping against the orb's side rumbled through the orb, the squelching sound began. As the trickle became a flood that seemed to go on forever, she shivered and trembled within, watching. The thought of them covering her, devouring her, and taking her life from her was so frightening that she was shaking uncontrollably throughout her ordeal.

The blunt, dry, drawn-out sound stroking her fingers across her orballoon made was magnified a hundred times. The short, sharp hisses, overlapping as their jostling bodies crowded against each other like an angry wave, forced her to shut her eyes to block the vision of them out and hold her hands over her ears as she tucked her head down towards her chest. She tried thinking of another dark, dank place which was not scary, to distract her from her ordeal.

Her dad occasionally took her with him when went on day trips to see the West Kennet Long Barrow and other places of interest in Wiltshire with his university students. While he taught fine art at Rowanshire University, as a secondary subject, he specialised in British folklore and pre-historic sites.

She remembered the cool, dark burial caves, where people went to drum, chant, meditate, or listen to talks on the site's history. He had taken her on official guided tours as well, and they borrowed her uncle MJ's campervan a couple of times and spent weekends in the area. The first time she had gone with him, they had also gone to Stonehenge. She had walked around the enormous stones, then darted between them and through the centre when the security people were looking the other way. She smiled at the memory briefly and opened her eyes.

She immediately closed them again when she saw that the snakes continued to cover her orb-shield. *Just how many were there?* Her thoughts then turned to Andrew, and she wondered what he would make of her predicament. She wished he were there with her.

Andrew, her friend, slash, possible boyfriend in Saint Lucia, was an adventurous, inquisitive, sensitive boy, who enjoyed telling her the story of how his parents had known they were meant to be together forever when they were only a couple of years older than they were, and had promised to make it official when they were old enough. Although they lived on opposite sides of the world, their affection for one another remained true, and they were committed to their long-distance love. She knew it was a slight exaggeration in geography, but it added a romantic element to their story when he explained it this way.

Although they were not related, the Vincent's, the James's, and the Franklyn's were close and all good Catholics. The Vincent family home was two houses down from the James family home and six houses down from the Franklyn's, Tyrone's family home in the town of Soufriere.

When the Vincents and the James's moved to England, they returned almost every year to Saint Lucia during the summer holidays. Andrew's mum and dad had known each other practically all their lives, in much the same way she and Andrew now knew each other and played together during the school holidays like them. Andrew's parents were always chilled out, easy-going and happy. His mum, Aunty JJ, was a yoga instructor, and Uncle MJ, her twin brother, ran a retreat next door with his new wife. She wondered whether Tyrone had asked JJ the same question Andrew had asked her all those years ago and how she might have answered him.

Back in the game ...

Unexpectedly, a strange feeling came over her, and she began to feel lighter, as though the layer of her energy, which reacted to outside stimulation, had been gently drawn away until nothing existed outside of the orb-shield. Her hands dropped from her ears. The sounds outside had lowered considerably, she was no longer sweating, and her skin was cool. She wondered at the strange sensory changes, and instinctively closed her eyes as a strangely familiar image began forming in her mind. A cloaked figure, mysteriously manipulating a set of strange rings, strengthened in intensity, and she heard the voice of the one she knew to be the Timekeeper.

For nine minutes, in their low, monotone voice, which was comforting and reassuring, they were telling her a story, speaking of things that seemed familiar but, at the same time, unfamiliar ...

In the Realm of the Empress, the sun turns slowly within its colossal symbol of the feminine, Venus, casting a myriad of colours across the sky. The combined, never-ending wind and the natural tone of the Empress, a high-pitched, chiming bell, indicates all is calm and at peace within the realm. The rustle of tree leaves, the sighing of night bloom petals and the swish of tall grasses brushing the air add to these two distinctive constants within the realm.

The Realm of the Empress is a realm of wonders beyond human imagination. Possessed of a meticulous, spiritual harmony and so magically different from the human physical realm, the closeness of the two realms would surprise many and, perhaps, be unbelievable. All within this realm possess magic, which is as normal and as common as say, the people of the earth having two feet.

Within this realm that is not so far away, from the moment she came into being within the cradle, the Empress Salliniquai had one of the four green-eyed, androgynous beings with features more feminine than masculine by her side. It fell to these ageless companions, who were blessed with powers and abilities of extraordinary range, to watch over her and guide her through her natural evolution in preparation for the tough challenges she had to face both before and after sacrificing herself to the Distance during the Offering.

It was the Alchemist who initially nurtured her with their caring hands and grace. Then she studied the realm's fields under the Awakener's tutelage. Once she learned her lessons with them, she spent time with the Timekeeper, learning to shimmer into and out of the seen and the unseen, among other things. Her final lessons, under the direction and care of the Elevated One, supported her evolving her femininity into that of a mature woman.

From the perspective of humans, Salliniquai appears as a young, immature girl of around sixteen earth years and, due to her rash, unthinking, short-sighted actions, all may believe this to be the case for once awakened, articulate and aware, Salliniquai proved to be a stubborn and demanding young lady, with a regally superior attitude.

Inside one of the three geodes of the Elevated One, the instructive Awakener and Salliniquai, the Empresserial student. Both superior entities of advanced spiritual intelligence, were involved in an argument. Stop. One moment, for we are in error. It was not an argument; it was a discussion. Yes, a discussion. One must never be so bold as to argue with Empress Salliniquai.

Having learned the art of wordplay well, she liked to have fun with the Awakener when she was in a mischievous mood. She used her wiley ways to twist them around her little finger, taking a cheeky enjoyment of their discomfort when they became torn between doing as she commanded and trying to do what was best for her. Determined to get her own way, Salliniquai used this advantage and was flower petalled to the earth, where she joined her energies with a young girl from the county of Rowanshire called ...

Sally opened her eyes and blinked three times in quick succession. "What an amazing story, Timekeeper." She murmured in a daze. As her senses aligned to her current surroundings again, all memory of the Timekeeper left her. "This Salliniquai sounds like a bit of a handful. I wonder who she is?" she murmured as she looked around. It seemed to have taken an age for all the snakes to pass over her, but eventually, the slithering, slapping sounds gradually became less intrusive, less creepy, and the hissing faded away. Finally, when the last of them disappeared down the long corridor and around the corner, she took a long deep breath, relieved.

She stayed within the orb-shield for an extra second or two, watching and listening for any sign of them coming back. When she could no longer hear the slithering, slapping sounds, she took another deeply calming breath. Her confidence returning, she knew she would have to venture out of the orb-shield and its protection soon. Time was of the essence, and the clock was ticking.

It was the faint, tick-*tick*, tick-*tick*, tick-*tick* sound from the unseen clock that got her moving again. She reached down to gently touch the cat's collar, and as she did so, the orb-shield faded, then vanished into thin air. She was immediately hit with the foulest of smells, much stronger this time. Standing up, she tucked the cat's collar securely into her pocket, then looked around for a minute. A long, deep, dreadfully menacing hiss carried along the tunnel, making the hairs on the back of her neck stand on end.

"Oh, my gosh. If that is the master snake, it sounds like a big one! I bet it's just waiting for its chance to get me too..." Her first mistake must have allowed only those milk snakes to get loose. If she makes another, would she release the master snake, or would she be faced with another sort before the big one? "...Oh, I wish someone were here to answer me," she muttered, frustrated. There was no one, of course. She alone had to find a way to outsmart the slithering beasties.

The snakes had left a thick, dark green goo in their wake. It sunk in between the cracks that roughly marked out the squares on the ground and all over the squares themselves. Her lip curled in disgust as, on checking the map, she saw that she would have to walk through it to reach the next die face. Her lips compressed together in grudging determination as she started along the corridor, heading deeper into the game.

Meanwhile, observing the game from their prime positions, Saxon and Noxas considered Sally.

"So far, she's doing good." Noxas proclaimed softly.

"So far, so good, yes. I never dreamed we would be honoured to participate in the Empress's elevation training." Saxon mused thoughtfully.

Noxas's brow tightened. "Brother, I don't think our game is part of her training. Not for the Offering at the Distance."

"No?"

"No. This feels more like ... a test of sorts. A trial, maybe? Because there is no kurren-see exchange. I wonder how her presence affects the other children and the longevity of our purpose."

"Very little, I hope. The energies of the ones we have brought to our Leap Year games, the ones chosen to lead during the new age, should continue to be magically protected, regardless of the outcome of this game."

"I have faith it is as you suggest, brother. Your faith in the Malsimily remains true. As does mine."

"It can be no other way, brother. Ahh look. She is almost at the next die ..."

Turning back to their view of Sally in the game, they watched expectantly.

Hurrying through the winding, uneven tunnel, she slowed and froze when she heard another deep hiss. They seemed to be coming with more regularity now, and she tried to dechiper in which direction the sounds were coming from, but she could not tell. A heavy, shifting sound, as though a beast of a size she could not imagine was moving through the game with calculated stealth, echoed from all around her once or twice, but it was impossible to determine which direction the sounds were coming from. She could be walking towards it for all she knew, but she had no choice if she was to continue following the map's directions.

The game was getting decidedly creepier, and although she was moving steadily, it felt far too slow. She paused and listened at every turn or curve, fearing to come upon either the hundreds of milk snakes or the master snake itself. She eventually reached the next die face, which showed a four. She shook her head, sighing in resignation as she pondered her next move. She could not afford to make another mistake as, according to the map, there were more die faces to get through. She bit one side of her bottom lip, twisting them to one side slightly. She could not make up her mind. She was dithering.

She was learning to accept this trait of her Libran nature, and the game was the perfect test of her ability to make a choice quickly. She suddenly thought of her unique little book, The Serenity Experience, and the confidence it brought her. Since reading it, she had noticed how she gradually began looking at things slightly differently. She had grown better at making decisions in general, even if they were small, insignificant ones, and she was a lot more confident when deciding which activities to get more involved in and which after-school clubs to join. Each time she made a firm decision, she grew more confident in herself and her capabilities.

Standing on the square before the die face in the wall, she took the second, enlarged pencil from the pouch and, without hesitation, thrust it through the hole on the bottom left. Instantly, something clamped bone grippingly tight around her arm, and she cried out in pain. The square below her feet and the wall the die was cast in rumbled and shook as a crusty, scraping noise echoed through the tunnel. Her arm was stuck again. She tried wrenching it out and could not. She began to panic as everything around her, except for the die face her arm was stuck in and the square she was standing upon, fell away. The ground and wall began to shift and revolve around, and she was suddenly lifted, up and away.

Oh no. Wrong again!? A feeling of dread crowded into her, and chilling goose bumps rose on her arms as the familiar, cold finger of fear raced down her spine.

6

Everything was blurred as she closed her eyes tight and gritted her teeth. Quite impossibly, she seemed to be moving in all directions at once, frighteningly fast. Ducking and dipping, juddering, and shaking so hard her teeth chattered. She continued to grit her teeth and kept her eyes shut, her nerves on edge and jangling. It was like being on a topsy-turvy waltzer at the fun fair. The one ride she did not like! Or like the dark, rolling water slide at the Dome.

The seconds seemed to stretch out as she thought of the day out she had enjoyed with her friends, which seemed so long ago. She had taken ages to decide what to wear while Hannah and Hope waited for her, trying not to be impatient. In the end, she had worn her light blue denim dungarees over a pale pink, short-sleeved sweater, and pink trainers.

Hannah, ridiculously cute with her permanent dimples, perfect teeth, and almond-shaped eyes behind black-framed glasses, looked cool as usual in her not quite, mismatched outfit of a Bob Marley legend t-shirt and a long, flaring skirt with squiggly Indian writing and dancing shiva's decorating the otherwise plain, thick cotton material. She had styled her hair atop her head in a ring comb.

Hope, all fresh-faced and pretty, had worn a fetching purple tracksuit with the top tied around her waist. Her hair was loose, and her cheeks were rosy. Their completely different styles suited them both, and unlike her, both would have chosen what to wear and thrown it all on in minutes. They never seemed to dither when deciding what to wear. She had no idea why she was thinking about this now, then realised it was to distract herself.

Back in her bedroom ...

"Ahh, I digress. The thought of you two distracted me, but it was the long, dimly lit, watery tunnels we jumped into at the water park I meant to think of. The tunnels that twist and turn, rolling us upside down and from side to side in a scary, uncontrollable fashion. That is what it felt like ..."

"Mm-hm..." Hannah murmured, continuing to draw.

Back in the game ...

Eventually, she realised she was moving on a diagonal. An upwards diagonal. Which should mean ... yes! She had chosen correctly! It must be a kind of spiralling, twisting ladder. She was safe, for now anyway. Just when she thought she would scream or throw up, the sensation of movement began to slow and then stabilise. Before stopping completely, she caught sight of the giant clock face. 10.15 pm. Abruptly, the die face released her arm, her knees buckled beneath her, and she sat down hard on the floor.

She considered the state of the pencil, still gripped tightly in her hand. It had remained whole. So, if she picked the right die hole, the pencils were not halved. Good to know. Although, if she had been paying attention and had not dropped the other one, she might have realised this earlier.

On this new level, the corridor was pitch black. She stood still for a while, waiting to see if her eyes would get used to the complete blackness, but after long moments, nothing changed. A sudden pressure on her thigh reminded her of the Cat's collar and its uses. Digging it out, she fastened it around her wrist this time.

A glowing emerald-green orb about half the size of a football appeared at once, hovering a few inches above the back of her wrist. She gasped, her smile brightening her mud and grime-stained face. She moved her hand in a flowing, figure-eight gesture, and the orb moved with her, bound by an invisible, magical field. Holding her arm with the orb-light attached out before her now, she squinted and peered into the impenetrable black.

Although the entire passageway was shrouded in shadow, the orb glowed bright, easily lighting her way. Steadily, she moved through the passage. It was a circular shaped tunnel with rough tree bark on its walls, and roots and vines crisscrossing the floor. She wondered, with dread, whether the tunnel represented the actual size of the master snake.

"It's probably slithered through this tunnel a million times." She mused softly, swallowing deeply. The tunnel was a foot or two taller than her but at least six times her width. "It could be a very, very, very big snake indeed," she murmured.

The slime, seeming to come from the walls itself, dripped down the uneven surfaces and cracks in dark runnels, forming a narrow river at the curvature's lowest, most central part. She was standing in the slime up to her ankles, and the horrible, pungent aroma was much stronger there, even though she knew she was higher up on the game's board. She took the map from her pocket and unfolded it quickly. It had transformed itself in places to reflect the level she was on. She wondered how many levels there were, then tried to think back to when she first saw the three-dimensional structure.

Back in her bedroom ...

"So, it hadn't looked like there were more than three or four levels to pass through," she explained to her two pals. "But I didn't trust the board was behaving according to my own common sense of playing."

"Good call, Bubblelicious," Hope said, thoroughly engrossed in the adventurous story.

"There wasn't a spiral staircase on the map or in the frame I saw at the beginning, but from what I experienced, it could be nothing but a spiral staircase. A wildly spinning spiral staircase, but a spiral staircase just the same. There were obviously hidden aspects to the game, so I couldn't take any of what I saw for granted."

"Uh-huh," Hannah murmured, drawing away, her strokes long and elegant.

"Again, very smart, Bubblelicious," said Hope.

Back in the game ...

Sally sighed. "Oh well, regardless of my suspicions, it's now after ten, and I have to ..." she paused. What was that? Had she heard something? A heavy, shifting sound? She turned around quickly, swinging her arm out before her so the orb-light cast its glow back the way she had come. Nothing. Then, something. A movement. Far, far back in the shrouded, endless dark. She saw ...

Eyes. Wicked eyes ... The eyes of a snake ... watching her.

For a long moment, all she could see was their malevolent glow in the darkness. They were so mesmerising she became pinned and transfixed to the spot, unable to tell how far away the snake was or whether it was still or moving. Blinking hard two or three times, cleared the hypnotising effect. Then she began to back away, slowly. She folded the map and returned it to her pocket, slowly. Were the eyes moving? Coming towards her now? She still could not tell. Making a quick decision, she turned quickly with one thought in mind ... Run.

Unfortunately, running through the tunnel was quite impossible, as she was hindered by thick roots and springy vines looking like they had grown so tangled with the specific purpose of catching and trapping ill-placed feet. She had to go carefully. A fall now might be the end of her, as the roots and vines would hold her fast until the snake arrived to chow down on her. She searched desperately for the next die face as she struggled through. Relief flooded through her at the sight of it, and she ran up to it, jumping over the last of the vines. Panting shallowly, she faced the five holes as she frantically grabbed the pencil from her pocket, fear clinging tight and terrifying to her. Without looking back or dithering about which whole to push it into, she jammed it into one of them—the top right.

The square upon which she stood immediately tipped upwards, dropping her ungraciously through a trap door. She dropped the half pencil and screamed as she fell, down, and down into the darkness of the snake's pit. She thought briefly of another of her mother's sayings *from the frying pan into the fire*. She had escaped being caught by the snake but was falling right into the pit. She had chosen wrong. Again. A long, dreadfully angry hiss followed her progress as she dropped through the trap door. Gravity did the rest ...

Somehow, she was not falling as freely as she thought she should be. She was so relieved at her luck in escaping the snake that it took her a moment to wonder how she did it. She appeared to be falling through a long, stale-smelling stocking of pale skin! The fall was, at first, smooth, but then it became bumpy. As she slipped and swung from side to side, she unfastened the collar from around her wrist, almost dropped it but snatched it back before it fell away and, sighing irritably, held it tight in her other hand whilst reaching around herself to clasp it around her leg. She managed it with a grunt of effort, and the orb-shield immediately materialised around her, a magical force inside keeping her upright within. Much better, she thought, looking through the skin of the orb at the sight rushing towards her.

Within seconds, with a long, wrenching tear, the orb burst out of the end of the master snake's discarded, fleshy skin. Her heart stopped at the breathtakingly sudden drop as the orb emerged above a cavernous pit. Huge flakes of dried scales floated around her as she plummeted towards the floor, which was a writhing, wriggling, disgusting mass of living death. There were hundreds, maybe thousands, of slick, poisonous snakes of several species, with no prey to pursue but her, and she was falling right into their midst. As scared as she was, she managed to keep her head. At least, she thought, until she crashed into them.

Fortunately, quite unbelievably, she did not crash. About a meter or so before reaching the snakes, the orb stopped abruptly and then dropped down with a lot less crash than she had feared. She did not understand how, but was very glad of it. Suddenly released from the orb's invisible force within, she instinctively dived into a high forward roll and kept rolling, using her momentum to push the orb forward whilst trying not to look at the scene around her. When she finally reached a wall at the side of the pit, she remained crouched, head down, shaking uncontrollably. Hugging herself tightly in shock, rocking backwards and forwards, her breaths were gasped and shaky.

She had no clue how much time passed before she felt brave enough to look out at her surroundings properly. She squinted and peered through the skin of the orb at the horrendous situation she was in. She saw no sign of the master snake and supposed it was because it was back on the level she had fallen from. The more her eyes got used to the dark, however, the wider they grew with terror.

From within her small enclosure, she stared through the membrane wall and tried to see if there was a way out, but there was nothing resembling an exit. It was dark and dank everywhere she looked, and although she could not smell anything, she knew it was monstrously smelly down there. Plumes of slow-moving, dewy mist wafted from cracks and crevices in the walls while a continually blowing breeze carried its stench to other areas in the game. After what seemed like hours but was only minutes, she resigned herself to thinking that maybe this was the end. That she had lost, and there was no hope.

Hope? The Juggernaut. Sitting in the dark pit, cocooned, and sweating within the orb-shield, she thought of Hope and her family of fitness freaks. The word freak meant in the positive sense.

***

A note from the Timekeeper. Generational friends ...

The three young girls had always been close. Their parents were friends for years, so they regularly got together for BBQs, birthdays, and other social occasions. On one such occasion, Simone and Hope's mum, Daphne, were discussing the new business she and her husband were setting up. Up until two years ago, Daphne, a tennis pro in her own right, had been working as a private tennis coach at a country club and some of the large, private residences of affluent families, most of whom lived in the North district of Rowanshire—the posh part of the county. Having secured lucrative contracts to teach their young, out of shape, often unwilling, spoilt, largely untalented and naturally uncoordinated, surly teenage offspring how to master the game, not because they genuinely had an interest in tennis, but because it was the done thing, took patience, tolerance, and tight-lipped endurance, on her part.

After seven years of this, Daphne could endure it no more. Fortunately, the work had served its purpose, for the remuneration for private coaching in this neighbourhood was quadruple what she considered reasonable payment. She did not argue with the figure or hesitate in accepting the first client, knowing word would spread and she would inevitably be in demand, as they each tried to outdo each other. Playing tennis was, to them, simply another way to show off the family's status and wealth. This generosity, however, allowed the Hallertons to save the money required to start their own physiotherapy business in a far shorter time than they had expected.

"Daph, you have the patience of a saint working with such hollow people." Simone had commented.

"But worth every penny, ay Simms? And hey, who am I to

complain if they decide I am worth paying that much?" She responded, shrugging.

Like their parents before them, the trio of girls' friendship was an important part of their lives. Sally gained strength from her friends and was often directed by their actions, even though it did not look that way to others, like her dad. He saw her as the linchpin in their friendship, and maybe he was right. But her contribution to the friendship was much more than simply that. She did not have something of her own, either life-changing or career-making, to direct her energy and commitment towards like her friends both did. So, their friendship was her focus, and she liked the responsibility of being the linchpin, though it really was a three-way, equal thing with all three contributing loads to the friendship.

Back in the game ...

Defeated and exhausted, she sat with her arms wrapped around her knees inside the orb-shield at the bottom of the dark, stinky pit. As she stared out at her horrible surroundings, unsure of what to do, her eyes glazed over briefly, her breathing calmed, and the strange whispering voice returned, speaking directly to her soul. The same sense of calm she felt the first time she was protected within the orb-shield returned. Ready for what was coming this time, she welcomed the feeling. She was grateful for anything that took her attention away from the pit, if only for a few minutes. She was taken off to another place, far, far away, as the feeling of weightlessness and a dreamy, comforting sensation embraced her, drawing her into a cocoon of distant memories ...

In the magical Realm of the Empress...

In the Cradle, where the Alchemist resides, the ceiling and the walls were as black as night, with enchanted lava showing through millions of thin, snaky cracks, offering a warm, orangy-golden glow throughout the solid rock. Lighting and drying areas within the cavernous space, the Cradle would have been decidedly dingy had it not been for the magical energy infused within its walls.

The Alchemist, a dark brown, soft-featured being with close-cropped golden-black hair, was sentimental, spoke in soft, nurturing tones, and was bound within the boundary of the Cradle. Their precious amulet, of the feminine symbol of Venus, was hand-sized and hung just below their solar plexus on the outside of their robe made of seven layers in a barely there material so fine and wispy, it fluttered and billowed out around them when they were in motion, giving the appearance of a smooth, floating gait. They wandered about barefoot and naked beneath, their body never entirely revealed through the layers.

When the Alchemist spoke in certain tones, their voice had the power to heal. Deeply penetrating, they could attune to the five senses of living beings and the realm's energy. Their three healing orbs, which were always close by, hovered above their head, and when they called forth their power in addition to their own, it initiated a healing process that, in the way of the Malsimily, entered via the seven chakras points to carry out its healing functions on the energy level required.

The Alchemist, while deftly gathering their billowing, multi-layered robe around them as they led the Timekeeper towards the large dais beyond the far end of the cavern's gushing waterfall, said,

"Thank you for coming, Timekeeper. We sensed the Empress's

energy was in distress and wanted to ensure the Kee was properly grounded as it is her only protection during her trial. We sensed something similar earlier, but then she seemed to calm down. Her distress, this time, is much more potent. Bringing her sixth sense here with your help was the only way we knew to bolster her strength."

Sho-linga, the Alchemist's huge snow-white karm, padded after them, then sat watching as they climbed the handful of steps up to the dais. The altar they paused in front of had a large, emerald-green symbol of Venus in a position of prominence upon a central stand.

The Timekeeper looked towards the symbol of Venus and nodded.

"We can show you where she is through the symbol of the feminine." The fact of their earlier interference was kept to themselves as the fingers of one hand began to work their time translation rings in a particular fashion. Their other hand touched the symbol gently with a single, ringed finger.

"Can we reach her without displacing the timeline?"

The Timekeeper nodded once again. "Indeed, we can. A gentle sleep spell within her dream should suffice."

"Marvellacious. We shall show her aspects of the realm, and then later, she must be encouraged to use the knowledge and infuse her work with the artist Hannah. Once the Kee is fully activated, she shall become ..." they paused, searching for the right word.

"Obsessed?" offered the Timekeeper in their usual monotone.

"Hm ... No. We were going to say focussed. But obsessed fits the attitude required just as well."

"In terms of sharing this realm's beauty, love, and healing with the world, the Sally host shall feel the strong draw towards this path. Her natural abilities shall be her strengths, and her determination will bring the wonders of the realm to the people of the human physical realm."

The Alchemist smiled gently, "It is as you say. Can you show me the path the Kee shall take her on as they mature?"

"We can. For her generation has been charged to progress the world towards The Third Way."

***

In the human physical realm...

Back in the game ...

Time and reality as a physical presence, both within and without the orb, faded away, and for nine minutes, Sally was in a beautiful place filled with magical wonders. Flying within a gigantic orb, she looked around at these fantastic wonders with a sense of joy and achievement. Moving towards a sun that never set but turned within an enormous, gloriously radiant symbol of Venus, she passed over the various fields letting her sweeping gaze take in the huge, smoky Rain bows rising from and thumping down into the ground, giant trees with massive, mattress sized leaves, a field of ice diamonds, their jagged uneven points jutting out from a sea of ice, a field of purple night blooms swaying in the light breeze, and a vast, upright ocean with no barrier of any kind holding it back, along with other familiar sights of pure wonder.

A two-fold sound she could not describe was a constant, and she somehow knew it was the never-ending wind and the tinkling chime of the Empress, whose realm it was. She could smell Raynorlorium and coconut and sensed the presence of magic in the air, which appeared to be everywhere and quite normal. She was comforted by the dream vision as it was a familiar, friendly place she could draw strength from, just like she drew strength from her friends.

"The Realm of the Empress," she whispered in awe. "The Realm of the Empress?" she repeated in her normal voice. She opened her eyes fully as a new sense of strength and determination rose within her.

Back in her bedroom ...

"What was strange, was that while I was sitting in the worst, most dangerous place in the game, I had a dream of another place. Considering where I was, it shouldn't have been possible, but I think I fell asleep for a minute or two."

Hope gasped, disbelieving, "You fell asleep?!"

"Yeah, but listen, I had the most amazing dream vision in those few minutes. Remind me to tell you all about it, Hannah. What I saw would make the most wonderful paintings. It feels like it could be something really important, as well."

"Why's it so important?" Hope asked immediately.

"I don't know yet. I just know it is. I also know *one hundred per cent* that you will want to paint what I saw." She spoke those few words with a passionate conviction Hannah had not heard from her before. She stared at her for a moment, eyeing her carefully. She was, of course, immediately intrigued.

"In that case, I can't wait!" she said, tucking a foot beneath her to get more comfortable.

"What you dreamed you saw, you mean?" Hope pointed out.

"Yeah, yeah, okay. Right, where was I?"

"What's a dream vision, Sal?" Hannah asked, her tone slightly urgent.

"It's..." she hesitated. "... a bit too complicated to explain now."

"But what if you forget it like all the rest?" She persisted.

"I won't. Besides, dream visions stay with you."

Hannah frowned. "How do you know that? You've never had one. What if ...?"

Sally looked at her patiently. "Honestly, they do. Trust me. So, there I was, having snapped out of it ..."

"You mean, you woke up from the dream, inside the dream," observed Hope in a gently mocking tone.

After a long pause, she shrugged dismissively, "Exactly. Then, rather than sitting in an almost blind panic biting my fingernails, I thought of Hope, who I knew if she were there, she would find a way out. If it were you, you would roll around to every corner of the pit if you had to, to escape. The Juggernaut would never baulk at such a challenge."

"Radically right, Bubblelicious," her friend agreed proudly. She was lying across the bed, squeezing one of her muscle-strengthening contraptions open and closed in one hand.

Back in the game ...

Damn, did she just drop off? At a time like this?

Speaking softly, she mused, "If I did, then wow, what a majorly cool dream vision. I wonder what Hannah will make of it? Maybe she could paint bits of it if I explained them." She sighed. "But first things first. I have to get out of this pit." She rubbed her eyes, and her gaze cleared. Her eyes suddenly widened. Could it be? Is that a ... a die face? She sat up straight, straining to see better.

A familiar square shape stood out in the murky wall on the far side of the pit. It was faded, stained, and crumbled around the edges, but there was no mistaking what it was. The face of a die! How had she not seen it before?

YESSS! A way out... maybe... Desperately hopeful, a rush of adrenaline began to pump through her veins. She wished she could make her orb fly to it through the air above the horrid little things. But such an action was impossible. She knew that such a thing was only possible in the Realm of the Empress. And she definitely wasn't there now.

What would she do if she were Juggs? How would she move if she were Serenity?

Remembering that the big clock ticked on somewhere in the game, slowly, with cat-like grace, she shifted onto all fours, then, reaching forward, tentatively pushed the orb's skin to test it. It gave a little, then rocked slightly. With more momentum, she pushed harder, and it wobbled and then began to roll. As she rolled the orb over and over, wobbling from side to side as she bumped over the mass of twisting bodies beneath her, she kept her eyes focused on the die face as she scrabbled forwards like a gerbil on a wheel.

She gained traction with her feet, and the orb gained speed. Panting, trembling, and giggling almost hysterically as she progressed, she worked hard to keep the orb upright and going in the right direction. Though it remained impregnable, rather than rolling like a ball, the base of the orb flattened and depressed a little, revealing the shapes of the snakes and giving her a feel of the squishiness of those she rolled over. Still, she was not frightened. Somehow, instinctively, she knew that nothing could break through her magical orb.

Now that her escape was within reach, she whooped and screamed with exaltation. She was nervous but full of adrenaline and raring to go on.

She tried not to think about the faint hissing, squelching, snapping sounds and did not look at the mass of snakes slithering and writhing beneath her with flicking tongues that spat poison. Her task was not easy, and she was winded when she reached the opposite side of the pit and the die face. When she saw the number of holes displayed, she exclaimed joyfully, *Juunes-strayaiah!* and barked gleeful, hysterical laughter at the single dark dot facing her in the centre. A huge, overwhelming relief flooded through her, accompanied by a slow, satisfactory, happy sigh.

It's a one! A ONE! Oh, what luck, what luck! She reined in her excitement when she realised that she could not poke it from inside the orb. She would have to dismiss the orb first, then use the die face. Her heart sank as she considered her chances. Some of the snakes were beginning to bump against the orb. It all depended on what happened when she activated the die. She knew it would be a ladder of some kind, but how fast would it appear? She still had another level to get through as well. She did not have time to worry about the snakes; she needed to escape the pit. Again, she was grateful the master snake was out of the pit, slithering its way elsewhere in the game in its search for her.

She pulled the hood of her catsuit over her head and it transformed into an all-in-one again. Taking the last pencil from her pocket, she readied it in her right hand and touched the cat's collar with her left. The orb faded, then vanished, and the overpoweringly foul stench of damp, festering nastiness, snake muck and slime hit her like a physical blow. In the same instant, the sounds in the pit magnified a hundredfold. It was deafening and booming and terrible. A second later, she was jamming the pencil into the dot and refastening the cat's collar securely around her wrist.

A light appeared from an impossibly high position, shining directly onto her upturned, desperately relieved face. It bore down on her from so far up she bent back a bit to see it. The descending ladder dropped swiftly with three resounding clunks, releasing impossibly long lengths of the ladder that ended before her. She did not hesitate. Returning the whole pencil securely to her pocket, she reached for the ladder and quickly stepped on, kicking at the snakes beginning to curl sinuously around her feet.

Quickly, she began to climb. Impulsively, she hissed down at them angrily in the same way she had seen Serenity hiss at dogs and other cats in her territory, and for a moment, they seemed to hesitate. Then, perhaps sensing the threat from her was an empty one, they began to climb again. Although she was not wildly keen on heights, she climbed quickly, hoisting herself up the rungs. She momentarily shut her eyes tight, then looked up and focused on the square of light above her. She could not block out the sounds, unfortunately, and the higher she climbed, the worse they became, echoing over and over. It was maddening. She concentrated on counting the rungs to stop herself from looking down. Up and up, she climbed, not daring to look down, and glad for the glow of the orb-light as her steps took her higher and higher.

"Fifty-five," she counted aloud sometime later, out of breath and gasping. The trap door did not seem to be any closer. At rung seventy-five, she saw the large clock face again, fixed into the wall behind the ladder. 11.35 pm.

Oh gosh! Is that the time? She was desperately tired but continued to climb, more slowly now, however, then slower still until, at last, she had to stop and rest for a moment. Panting and breathing heavily, she held on tight to the ladder with her forehead resting against it, waiting for her breathing to slow. She had to rest, just for a minute.

The ladder wobbled. She felt a steady trembling and glanced down. Her eyes bulged in horror as, rung by rung, the ladder below her disappeared beneath the bodies of the snakes crawling and wiggling their way upwards. Up, over, and through the rungs, they were no more than eight or nine rungs below her feet. She gasped, paralysed in terror, staring disbelieving at the hundreds of horrors wiggling their way up the ladder toward her.

No English translation. Closest Malsimily term is - Mellotorium! she exclaimed. "You crummy little buggers." Springing into action, she no longer grappled her way awkwardly up the ladder but moved with an alacrity and smooth coordination the Juggernaut would have been proud of.

Back in her bedroom ...

"It wasn't *funny!*" She exclaimed irritably as Hannah and Hope rolled about laughing like it was the funniest thing they had ever heard at her description of the snakes and her subsequent springing into action.

"It so is." Hope's high-pitched peel of laughter was loud and unrelenting as Hannah's laughter eventually died away to low giggles, and then she urged,

"Go on, Bubbs, what happened next?"

Back in the game ...

The thought of falling back into the pit or being caught by the snakes gave her a further burst of energy. There would be no way of stopping the snakes from covering her, just as they covered the ladder. She climbed quickly, with a surety and skill more catlike than human, and for the second time since she had begun to play, she was really frightened by what was coming after her.

Somehow, she managed to keep a level head and concentrated on the climb. Then, at last, the trap door was within reach. The snakes, a mere two rungs below her now, seemed to speed up in their efforts to reach her. Kicking wildly and grunting with effort, she hoisted herself up through the trap door, awkwardly pulling her legs up and through after her, snagging and ripping one leg of her all-in-one. Once completely out, she hurriedly slammed the door shut and sat on it to ensure the snakes could not push it open from below. Her smile, though satisfied, was a bit bleak. No graceful, karm-like exit and landing this time, my friends, she thought. Way too close for comfort. Three snakes had managed to slither through in the second or two it took for her to slam the door closed. That was close. Very close. The snakes slithered away to her left while she sat in a heap on top of the door, panting hard.

7

She was back on the level she had been tipped down from, a short way away from the location of the die face. At least this time, she knew which of the holes on the five numbered face not to push her last pencil through. Somewhere behind her, the hissing had increased in volume.

"Now, I really can't afford to make another mistake because there's another die to go after this one." She cautioned herself. She retraced her previous steps the length of the tunnel over the roots and vines, through muddy goo again with her light held out in front of her, until she stood before the die face. Her choices were upper left, lower left, centre, or bottom right. "Oh, mellotorium, which is it!!" She shouted in a huff. She was annoyed with herself for getting annoyed and frustrated with the apparent unfairness of it all. She was tired, irritated, and just wanted the damn stupid dream to end.

Back in her bedroom ...

"Shhhh!" Hope hissed with a wide-eyed stare of surprise. "Trust your voice to return as you said that." She jumped up, rushed over to the door, and leaned an ear against it. "I hope your dad didn't hear you say that."

Sally glanced at her, frowning, "Say what?"

"You said, for em's sake, but properly, you know?" she strode back to the bed. "You'll be in trouble if your dad heard you."

"No, I didn't," she frowned. "I mean, you know I don't like swearing."

"But you did then. With the word fully articulated as well." Hope insisted, her tone hushed. She glanced at Hannah for backup, but Hannah's head was down, eyes fixed on her drawing pad. "Besides, it's no biggie, it is human nature. You should hear the language seasoned athletes use on the track and field."

"I was sure I said ... " Sally began, then, eager to finish the story, she replied a bit defensively, "If you say so. Now, can I get on with it?" Hannah looked up, caught Hope's eye, and raised her eyebrows at her quizzically. She put a finger to her lips and slightly shook her head. Hope bit back the retort she was about to offer and, flopping down onto the bed, began to stroke Serenity again.

Back in the game ...

Listening with a concentrated ear, Sally noticed the ticking had speeded up. Could this be because she was nearing the end? Maybe.

"Time for a lucky guess, I guess," she said out loud in a forced, cheery tone as she pushed the pencil into the lower left hole. She pulled the pencil back out when nothing happened to find it still complete. Where was the ladder? Suddenly, a hiss of seriously malicious intent reverberated around the passage, loud enough for her to freeze and tense up immediately. It grew deafening as it echoed around the tunnel while she waited. Nervously, reluctantly, unable to help herself, she looked over her shoulder, and at last, finally got to see the massive monstrosity in the flesh.

Its pattern of black diamonds stood out over shades of brown, identifying it an Adder. Slide-weaving its way almost drunkenly towards her, the snake filled the passage with its huge bulk as it moved between the outcrops and branches with smooth familiarity. Its hypnotising eyes glistened as they kept eye contact with her own, while its fangs, which were of epic proportions, dripped drops of poison the size of her hands.

Mellotorium! That thing would eat her alive in one snap of its jaws ... The stammering thought stuttered through her mind as she swallowed dryly and shrank back against the wall, eyes fearfully round and filled with dread. Now, she was utterly petrified and terrified of losing. Not so much the game, but her life by being eaten by the snake. Maybe that last hole was a dud. Maybe it was a red herring or something. Biting her trembling lower lip, with shaking hands, she turned back to the die face and tried a different hole. This one just has to be right. The snake was almost upon her and this time, she would die if she was wrong.

She shoved the pencil into the bottom right hole, and with fright and desperation etched on her face, she bravely turned to face the snake. She flinched and shrank back against the wall again, crying out in terror as it slowed and loomed before her. It widened its sticky jaws, and she could see right into the darkness of its deep throat. Before it could clamp its jaws around her, she felt a sudden jolt and with a loud boing, she was shot upwards on a spring like a jack-in-the-box. Instinctively holding her arms above her head, as Hope did when she was diving, she shot through a trap door that had opened above and got stuck there halfway through it.

Back in her bedroom ...

Hope declared nonchalantly. "There, see. I wouldn't have got stuck."

Sally gave an exasperated sigh. Hope had not stopped picking at her story. "As athletic and sporty as you are, you wouldn't have fitted through the trap door anyway. The snake would have eaten you, legs first. Now, can I finish, please?"

"*Soreeeee* ... " Hope rolled her eyes in an exaggerated fashion. But when she thought about being eaten legs first, an expression of discomfort crumpled her features.

"So, following that dive-leap ..."

Back in the game ...

She struggled to pull herself through, kicking and twisting violently whilst trying to see what the snake was doing. It reared backwards, preparing to eject a string of poison towards her. Desperately, she pulled her feet through, scraping her thigh painfully against the edge of the door, then quickly ducked back and away as a stream of thick globs of poison shot through the opening, missing her by inches. She scrambled forward to kick the door shut, then scooted away from the opening, her breathing ragged. Getting to her feet with her knees practically knocking, she was relieved the door was too small for the snake. There was another long tear in her catsuit, and she could feel a repeated pulsing on her thigh where a patch of skin, looking red raw and stinging like she was being stabbed with hundreds of needles, could be seen through the tear. The wound stung just like when Serenity had accidentally scratched her. Quickly, she unfolded the map to see where she was in the game. She was on the final level.

"Oh, thank God!" She exclaimed, desperately relieved.

On this last level, the hallway was the shape and size of a hallway at her school, except there were die faces all along it, with fist-sized holes as the dotted numbers in the walls. As she watched, a snake poked its head out of one of them, tasted the air with two flicks of its forked tongue, and then retreated. The same thing happened many times from many holes as she watched. None came out entirely, however, and she sensed their stealthy interest was their way of monitoring her progress, or they could be hiss-communicating exactly where she was to the master snake.

The ceiling and floor were a black, glassy substance, like the wall behind the till at the charity shop Hannah's mum managed, which was tinted on one side. She wondered if someone, or something, was watching her from behind it.

As the seconds stretched out in a strange, magical way, she thought of all the times the three had visited the charity shop. Inside, she always headed to the books section while Hannah rifled through the rows of donated clothes, looking for,

"Anything from the sixties and seventies era."

Hope had a big aversion to rifling through other people's cast-offs, as to her, it was hugely distasteful, whether it was dusty books hundreds of people had handled, old board games, or clothes from decades ago.

"Clearly, I don't understand the fascination," she would say, unable to hide her cringe-like demeanour.

"Hope, you do act the snob sometimes," Sally said over her shoulder.

"It's not an act. I'm simply an ordinary girl who literally likes ordinary *new* things, that's all."

"Ordinary? *You?*" Sally exclaimed. "Miss Olympian 2024, or is it 2028? I'd say you were, *literally*, more extraordinary than ordinary." Hope grinned at her. "And I'll be there in the stands cheering you on when the time comes."

"Me too," Hannah said, having just then joined them. She was carrying at least three items of clothing.

Hope wriggled her nose at her choices, then replied, "Fantastico. I'd expect no less of my two best friends." She draped an arm across Hannah's shoulders.

"You mean, your only two friends," Hannah mumbled.

"Yup, if you say so."

On one of those days, after she and Hope had gotten bored with pulling faces at the customers waiting to pay for their goods at the till, she stayed in the back room while Hope returned to the shop. As she stood there, a sudden glimmer of light caught her eye, coming from a large cardboard box on the floor opposite the back office. It was labelled *donate to specialist or chuck*. Curious, she went over to investigate and, kneeling beside it, looked in.

The box had several worn, faded, cheap-looking, well-thumbed books inside and a book titled *The Serenity Experience*, which was vaguely familiar. It looked new and had a strange glow, which flashed out at her. Reaching inside, she pushed the other books aside and, finding her prize, stared down at it for several seconds. As she did so, the Timekeeper chose that moment to manipulate time from somewhere beyond the human physical realm. Now infused with magic, the air began to thicken and swirl around her, and suddenly, everything stopped.

A magical moment of mystery no one else could see, hear, or

sense occurred for nine seconds. She heard a brief, tinkling chime and watched in fascination as a misty projection of sparkling, blue-hued light glittered brightly around the book for a moment. It blinked out when she reached out and touched it, and a shock of energy surged through her. Gasping softly, she drew the book towards her and clutched it to her chest. She looked around then, but no one else had noticed the unusual occurrence. Remembering where she had seen the book before, she saw it was by the same Author who had written *Astrology for your Astro child*, the book she had ordered from Serenity, her uncle MJ's shop, when she was nine. During the visit, the zodiac signs fascinated her and she wanted to learn more about them. While she waited for her mum to finish her visit with Uncle MJ, she had flipped through it and then asked if she could keep it. As it was the only one in the shop, her uncle had promised to order her a copy. The Serenity Experience, had been on one of the tables. As she reached for it, her uncle had picked it up first and said,

"Hey, not that one. It's a book for adults, my sweet."

"How long until I'm an adult?" she asked immediately.

Chuckling, he replied, "About another seven years."

Ha! Excellacious! She exclaimed almost wildly but at the same time, inwardly and quietly. She would not have to wait all them years after all. She was beyond pleased as she held the book protectively against her. Flushed with pleasure and trying to subdue her wide grin, she could hardly contain herself. A cursory flick through the pages revealed a single line of text on several pages, which she thought were the chapter headings and sub-headings. But then she read,

Warning: The knowledge in this book is restricted to persons aged sixteen and over. The Salliniquai host may read one or two choice sections, sentences, and about spiritual tools, but the rest shall remain untranslated.

The spiritual tools were interesting, unusual things she overheard her uncle discussing with her parents when he had been at their house. The book also included tasters from the third book in the series (True Malsimily. Translation Withheld - TM. TW).

Flipping to the back page, she found the Author's prediction, which read:

This book is the second in a series of three. The first, titled Spiritual Illumination, was published between the summer solstice of 1988 and the winter solstice of 1989. The second, The Serenity Experience, was self-published around the summer solstice 2019. The third book in the series, (TM. TW), shall (*High Malsimily, translation in progress* ...) between the leap years 2024 - 2028. For these are the years when the Third Way shall gather momentum. (TM. TW) will become the book of choice for women on spiritual journeys and for those who can embrace The Third Way.

Returning to the beginning, after reading the strong first line of the introduction in (TM. TW), she understood why the book was for adults. It read,

Growing up in southeast London in the seventies, racism was rife, the national front was strong, and one of my neighbours had a dog called the N-word.

A few months ago, when Hope, Hannah and herself had gone to Hannah's straight after school, Dyon and Douglas had got home late covered with cuts and bruises. They had been fighting with a group of white boys from another school who had called them this and other names. She had felt terrible for them, knowing they were not the type of boys to either start or back down from a fight.

Although she knew she might not understand all the information in the book, she was already intrigued and read on. She found another taster line from the book's introduction, which was much more positive.

As one of the feminine, you realise you are a Goddess, right? It began. What was strange was that most of the text was preceded by the words (Malsimily translation shield in place, due to age (of Aquarius, and the age of Empress Salliniquai's host) restriction) and seemed to be written in another language, until she got to another taster paragraph.

Deep inside, at the centre of your being, a warm, spiritually eternal force wants to build and rise through you. This was followed by something about a Great Suffering and the exact cautionary words as before (Malsimily translation shield in place, due to age (of Aquarius, and the age of Empress Salliniquai's host) restriction).

While confused by this, it felt like the book was teasing her by letting her see these few sentences. Then she wondered how the book could possibly know she was under sixteen, who the Empress Salliniquai was, what the Great Suffering thing was about, or who it was referring to when it mentioned a host.

Most of the text was indecipherable and seemed to be in a language her mind could not understand. Still, quite strangely, on another inner level, she somehow could. Except for the Spiritual tools' excerpts, practically all the information in the book was like this, and the text only became readable once she got to the Author's prediction, another excerpt from (TM. TW). *Indecipherable,* she chuckled softly to herself. Another word she managed to use in its proper context.

Although she instinctively understood that the book was being secretive for a reason, she was a bit gutted at having to wait until she was sixteen for the text to be revealed. How would she keep her excited anticipation tempered for three whole years? She had asked Hannah's mum if she could keep it, hoping and praying that she could. She was not sure she could leave it behind if not.

"I'll pay double whatever the price is for it." She offered generously.

"You won't understand most of it, Sally. It's kind of a spiritual book for women." She told her from where she stood in the office doorway.

"I know. I really like the cover, though. And MJ said it is never too early to start thinking about spirituality. I mean, it's really ..." The phone on the desk in the office behind her rang.

"Alright, take it. No payment necessary," she said, turning and reaching for the phone. Sally had tucked the book into her bag, a smile of relief on her face. She left a generous donation in the charity box by the till as payment.

Back in the game ...

Saxon and Noxas had watched her progress with an almost lazy interest until she escaped from the pit. Now, both were leaning forward eagerly, watching to see how she would finish the game.

About fifty feet ahead of her, the corridor opened into a vast, seemingly wall-less room. She ran towards it, staying close to the centre, trying to ignore the sudden rise in snake heads poking out of the die faces. Their numbers had multiplied considerably, with almost every hole now occupied with a snake's head, weaving about in a slow, hypnotic way, the sound of their hissing engulfing her. Her run to the end of the hallway had her panting again, and she was shaking a bit as she stood bent over with her hands resting on her thighs, trying to calm her breathing. She took in the view before her. One hundred illuminated numbered squares formed a flat grid on the dark ground, glowing eerily in the surrounding blackness. There appeared to be nothing but a dark gloom beyond the grid's edges, and the gridlines seemed to be made of a flexible substance, not attached to anything. They looked very unstable.

The end of the game. Oh, at last! Feeling something brush against her shoulder, she whirled around, expecting to see the snake at her back. She was surprised to find a balloon like the one she had at the beginning, but smaller, drifting beside her. She could see two palm-sized, square objects floating inside through the milky skin—two extra-large golden dice. The balloon burst then, and the dice hovered in mid-air for a moment, giving her time to grab them. As she did so, she gasped in surprise as she was lifted, up and over the grid in slow motion to land squarely on square ninety. She wobbled about and dropped into a crouch as the flexible square dipped and shifted under her weight. It was like trying to balance on a tightrope.

The six sides of the dice were numbered not with dots but with the faces of Saxon, the grinning boy on one, and Noxas's half-hidden big face on the other. She shook them awkwardly between her small, dirty hands and threw them to the ground. They tumbled away, faces interchanging as they turned over and over. Both landed on the last square, one hundred. The die with Saxon's face showed the number two face up, the other with the face of Noxas, a four. Square ninety-six lit up.

The clock had stopped ticking, and she worried again about the snake. It wouldn't be long before it tongue-sniffed her out and reached her. Was she safe where she was? Her green eyes darkened as a solid determination to succeed rose within her again. She could not, and would not, fail. She hunkered down briefly, then jumped with a momentum that carried her upwards and forwards. She landed safely but awkwardly in the middle of square ninety-six, hissing a sharp intake of breath as a sudden sting snapped across her right heel. Tears sprang to her eyes, but she wiped them away quickly as the dice popped up from the grid and flung themselves towards her. She caught them in both hands, then immediately threw them down again. The Saxon die showed a three, the Noxas die, a one.

"Yes! Yes! *Yes!*" she punched the air with her fist. Then wavered slightly as the squares of the grid began to shudder. Small cracks had started to appear along the dividing lines of the grid. As the ends of the flexible substance began to unravel, half of one of the grid squares to her side dropped through into the darkness below, while the square marked one hundred stretched away from her, then retracted back towards her. She had to decide when to jump by quickly judging the stretching squares. Briefly, she considered what might happen if she missed the square marked one hundred. With only seconds to decide, as had happened before during the game, these seconds seemed to stretch out, giving her time to think about a conversation she had overheard between her parents ...

Her dad managed to book their flights back to Saint Lucia, but he was a bit concerned with the responsibilities her mum would be taking on, as well as his own work. Luckily, the family home had four bedrooms, plenty of space, and a Wi-Fi connection, so he could work remotely in relative peace, easily keeping in touch with his students through Zoom and podcasts. She had been explaining that, yes, there were other members of the family there who could look after her mum. Four lived in the same town, but two of those worked full-time at one of the hotels as an administrator and a gardener. Another was a taxi driver who was always busy because he worked almost exclusively for one of the hotels. The other she did not include because he could not be relied upon.

"He's useless," her mum had said. "All he seems interested in doing is liming." Hanging out, in other words. However, on the plus side, one of the family was a doctor. Although he had a busy schedule working at the hospital in Vieux Fort, which was temporarily based in the old Olympic stadium, and running a surgery at the small medical centre in a village called Choiseul, he could visit his aunt often. Other relatives living in other areas of the island could swing by regularly, but Simone needed to be there to organise her care and these visits.

Thinking of this conversation, Sally was more determined to win the game. She was looking forward to returning to Saint Lucia for so many reasons, and nothing would spoil this chance to go back for her. *Nothing*.

While she played the game, an answer for Andrew had come to her, and she could not wait to tell him to his face what she had decided. Andrew, a year-and-a-half older than her, was six inches taller than her when they stood together in the summer. He seemed quite a bit taller when she saw him at the wedding a couple of weeks ago, and she wondered whether he would take after his dad and grow to over six feet tall. A confident boy with a teasing, cheeky smile, his highly infectious laugh was the same, and his humble humour still had her in fits of giggles.

In their last conversation, he had shyly and quite sweetly asked her an important question before she had flown back. Acting as cool as a cucumber, she had said she would think about it and let him know when she returned in the summer. She could not wait to tell him her answer now.

If she made it out of the game, she promised to make her confirmation at the Catholic church in Soufriere, too. She smiled inwardly at the promise. Her parents were Catholics, and while her mum attended church regularly, her dad only went occasionally. Since she turned twelve, her parents allowed her to choose whether she wanted to go. She never did, not in England anyway. In Saint Lucia, though, she attended church at least twice during the holidays, which pleased them.

There was a different feel to the Catholic services in Saint Lucia, apart from always being warm and airy inside the church. For one thing, the congregation dressed in their bright and colourful best rather than for warmth, which encouraged a more positive attitude towards worship. Going to church was a real occasion in Saint Lucia. Many of her friends went to church. Not every week and not because their parents sent them, but because they thought it was important. All the children she hung around with had been christened and had made their first holy communion, and she remembered how they joyfully celebrated these occasions.

That is IF she made it out of this. She sighed heavily, returning her attention to the business at hand. Square one hundred was the last square on the grid. She could see nothing beyond it except darkness. She crouched on all fours as the already unsteady ground shook again, more violently this time. More squares were shaken away from the grid. Biting her lip again, she tried to gage the distance to square one hundred, but she could not as it kept stretching away and coming back.

"Noxas, please, can you help me?" She begged, almost to herself. Noxas's strong and encouraging voice bellowed out from within the die, surprising her.

"Leap Sally! Leap like the leap year it is and like you have never leapt before! Reach beyond the one hundred." The die dropped away as the sides of that square began to crumble.

"Yes, you can do it, Sally, but you might not make it. Is it really, just a jump away?" Came Saxon's familiar, teasing voice from the one remaining die. "You can reach the one hundred easily. But hurry, the snake approaches." The die then tipped over the square's edge and fell away. At these last words, she could not resist turning to look behind her. She immediately wished she hadn't. The giant snake was rushing towards her so fast; she saw it only in a split second before turning back and leaping without hesitation, with all the spring and strength her legs would allow.

With her head thrown back, her eyes wide and wild, and her back arched in an elegant curve, as her arms stretched out to the ends of her fingertips, she reached forwards and upwards for extra lift. The downward curve of her leap happened in slow motion as she dropped toward square one hundred, but the smile on her face began to slide away, as incredibly, she seemed to have jumped just a bit too far, missing the furthest edge by inches. She began to drop down, and down, into the darkness. As she fell, she passed the giant clock face once more. 11.59. Faintly, she heard Noxas's voice echoing from somewhere below. He was chuckling, telling her she made it. She won fair and square. Fainter still, she heard Saxon referring to the Empress Salliniquai.

"Why, oh, why, do they always, always jump too far in the end?" Saxon asked Noxas.

"It's the sight of the snake rushing towards them like that. You warn them of its approach on purpose, don't you? Knowing they cannot resist a look. It must be pure fright which makes them leap so well in the end."

"Yes, I'm compelled to say it at the end of every game. But not all turn to look, Noxas."

"Luckily, Empress Salliniquai did."

"Which means she will make it safely out. Out as in properly out. Alive and well out ..." His tone was both regretful and relieved.

"Yes, all of the above." Noxas chuckled, amused by his words.

"A fitting end to a very fitting, very well-played game then. Right, brother?"

"Indeed, it is so. Although, if she had lost, we could not have kept her with us anyway. That kind of neglectful interference would undo our magical agreement. As she is of the True Malsimily, an agent of the supreme would have been sent to displace us. We would have faced dissipation, and all those we have taken, those who have a part to play in the human physical realm's divine future, who must survive the Great Suffering without mental disturbation, may have also been jeopardised.

"It is fortunate then that we had fun, and she has come to no harm. That call from the human physical realm was a strong enough pull to draw her back to her life."

"Indeed. Yes indeed. Although what will become of her once the Empresserial energy returns to her realm?"

"Sally?" he contemplated the question. "I imagine her destiny lies upon a different path now. One of global importance that will progress The Third Way." Their voices slowly faded away, back into the magical realm of the unseen.

8

Sunday 1st March, 2020

"And then I woke up." Sally finished with a shrug.

"Well, get you with your bad self. I would've loved to have played the game." Hope sounded a tad envious as she shifted to sit up on the bed.

"You're mad, Juggs. That kind of game's definitely not for me. I don't know how you did it, Sal." Hannah said admiringly.

"Well, I didn't actually do it. It was just a dream, remember? But oh, it felt so real."

"Those bruises you've got prove it was real. But I don't understand how that could be possible ..." Hope said with a curious, slightly confused expression.

"I'd rather not dwell on that aspect of it, it's too strange to get my head around at the moment." Hope nodded, but the look in her eyes showed she wasn't finished with the subject. Considering her own sporting activities, she knew all about cuts and bruises and found it strange that her friend had obtained them while dreaming. There must be a rational, normal reason for her getting them. It was a puzzle she would ponder, long and hard.

"I managed to do a few drawings from your descriptions," Hannah said, breaking into her thoughts.

"Cool. Let me see."

"Wait a minute. Are you sure that is all you remember of the whole weekend? There is nothing you left out?" Hannah asked.

"No. Not that I can think of. What about you two? Did we get up to anything else I should know about?" The two girls exchanged barely hidden, furtive glances. "Hey, what's that look between you?" her voice was concerned with what they could be hiding from her.

"Well, there was that one thing ..." Hannah began slowly.

"What thing?"

"It's quite embarrassing, really," said Hope, pulling a face.

"What is? What did I do?" She was sitting forward now.

"I'm not sure we should say. You might literally never go out in public again."

She frowned, her eyes widening, "Oh god. What did I do?"

They fell about laughing. "The look on your face is quality. That got you going, didn't it?" Hope giggled. Hannah let her off the hook.

"No, Bubbs, there's nothing else."

"We thought we'd wind you up a minute. There's nothing else to tell, is there Smudge?"

"Nope. Honestly, nothing else." Hannah confirmed, to Sally's relief.

She sent Hope a quick, unforgiving look. "Excellacious. Let's have a look at the pictures then." Pushing up from the wicker chair, Hannah crossed to the bed to sit between them. With a grand gesture, she flicked over the first page of her large sketchbook. The first picture was of the Clown. Although he was just an outline in black pencil, she had perfectly captured his energy behind the Clown get-up. She did not just draw the face, but the whole of him, flaring long coat, big nose, and everything. She had added a patch or two of colour in places so she would remember the colours Sally had mentioned when describing him.

"That's him. Are you sure neither of you saw him at the party?" She asked. Hannah shook her head.

"Nope, definitely not. I would've remembered." Hope said. The next picture was of Sally in bed, followed by a drawing of the party.

"This is the strange party," Hannah said, lifting the next page over. Sally and Hope glanced blankly at one another, then at Hannah. They could see only slanting lines, swirls, dots, and strange shapes, but nothing explicit or solid.

"Hmm ..." Hope mumbled doubtfully.

Sally cocked an enquiring eyebrow at her friend. "Um?"

"Sorry, yeah, you won't really understand this one. It's all in my mind how you described it. It won't make sense to you, but it's a technique I use when I need to draw many things in one place quickly. We'll skip it for now."

"Wow!" She exclaimed at the following sketch. "Han, that's totally marvellacious!" It was a three-dimensional snakes and ladders game, which she had taken the time to add colour to here and there. Some of the colours she took from Sally's description, others from the actual board game she had retrieved from under her bed, and leant it against it. The snake skin walls and the rising gooey substance from the first tunnel were next. Then, the orb-shield with Sally looking scared inside of it. A big shiny die face was next, with one dot in the centre. Then she had sketched a drawing of the big Adder and, finally, of the last part of the board, the end of the game. "I can't believe you drew all that, Smudge-face."

"Oh, how you underestimate my talents, Bubbs," she mocked. "I got a bit stuck on the last picture, so I just added bits from my imagination. I might use some of these in the future."

"Good for you. I'm just glad I remember it all now and have my voice back. Thanks for this, you two." She had returned to the real world alive and in one piece.

Hannah, a curious girl who usually noticed everything, had caught sight of the new addition to her bedroom. She closed her book and while reaching over to replace it in her bag, nodded towards the long, black, soft guitar bag leaning against the wardrobe door.

"Sal, before we go. What's in that?" her tone suggested that she knew what it was and wished to see it.

"Oh, you'll never guess." Her reply was exaggerated as she reached for it.

Hope, who was not musical at all and would not know a guitar from any other string instrument, asked innocently,

"That's too small to be a guitar. Is it a banjo?"

Hannah cracked up; her explosion of giggles infectious. "Of all the instruments you can think of ..." she gasped. Tickled by Hope's ignorance towards anything other than sports, Sally grinned in disbelief.

"A banjo?! What would I want with a flaming banjo?" Rolling her eyes, she laughed along with Hannah. She grabbed the bag, unzipped it, and slowly and carefully produced the shiny brown travel guitar.

"Wow!" Hannah gushed. "It's beautiful."

"Is it the one Snowboy gave you? I never knew you could play an instrument?" Said Hope. "Play us something."

"Hope, you're such a muppet. I've only just got it. I can't play anything yet."

"You're so funny. So funny." Hannah chuckled, almost rolling around again.

"I wasn't trying to be." Hope mumbled as Hannah nudged her playfully.

"I can't play anything, but look," she turned it around so they could see the back. Written in thick black pen were the words. *For Sally, with the green eyes. Play well, Snowboy.* Then, *Take care of her, sweet Sally. Trevor.*

"Oh my gosh! No way! An autographed guitar from Deep Silver Lining!!"

"And he'll still be there when we go back. He's promised me a lesson."

"Oh, Bubbs, you should video it and send it to us. It'll go viral." Hannah said.

She pressed her lips together and shook her head. "They've asked me not to do that, actually. Anything like that must go through their publicity office or something first, in case their location is accidentally revealed in the background. I didn't really get why. A protective measure for all concerned, they said."

Hope gushed enviously. "God, I'm soooo jealous. Not only have you met Snowboy in the flesh ..."

"And keyboard Trevor," Sally added.

"*And* keyboard Trevor," Hannah repeated.

"You've got a signed guitar, the promise of a private lesson, and you're going back to the Caribbean to hang out with your sweetheart while me and Hannah will be stuck here, shivering."

"Oi, Andrew's not my sweetheart!" She denied it hotly. *Not yet,*

137

anyway...

Hope gave her a long, doubtful look. "He should be. He's cute."

She rolled her eyes. For a moment, she almost told them the question he had asked her. She would, she thought, but not while Hope was teasing her about him.

"Sal's got a boyfriend, la la, la, la, la la..." Hope sang.

"Oh, *shut up*, Juggs. He is *not* my boyfriend. Shhhh, my dad's working."

"I wish I were going to Saint Lucia. It sounds so nature-filled, exotic, and totally radical. I bet I would love it there," she said wistfully. Hannah, exchanging a brief, knowing glance with Sally, chuckled further as she gathered her things together and stood.

"You're so funny juggs, and you don't even know it," she said softly.

"Why? What have I said now?" Hope grumbled.

Although she often wished, enviously, that she could go on holiday somewhere as exotic as Saint Lucia, her friends were not convinced she would like it. While there were many adventurous things to do, most people went there to relax, lie around in the sun, and enjoy great food, rum cocktails, and smoothies. The strength of the heat would be a test for her pale, freckled skin, and wouldn't she get bored being in a hotel for most of it? Although, if it had a gym, swimming pools, and a beach right in front of it, she could be kept reasonably busy. Hope was too charged up and energetic to enjoy doing nothing but slowing her pace right down, relaxing in the sun, and lazing around. Her family usually went to places in Scotland or Wales. Rambling holidays where they climbed peaks, took long, brisk walks through valleys, and enjoyed views of wide-open spaces with brisk winds blowing about them.

"Let's get some fresh air. We've been holed up in here for long enough." Hope suggested.

"Yeah, come on," agreed Hannah.

"Ok, let's go. Time is of the essence." Sally said.

"Time is of the essence? Where did you hear that?" Hannah asked, curious.

She shrugged. "From my mum, I think."

"Also, as you'll be jetting off to paradise tomorrow, we should be making the most of your last day," Hope said. "Which unfortunately counts me out because I have to get back. We're going to my nans for lunch; she lives miles away. Walk through the park with me?"

"Alright."

"Yeah, cool."

"*Cold* you mean," said Hope, ever the comedian.

"Whatever, let me put this away." Sally said, zipping the guitar carefully back into its case. "Right then, let's go." They noisily descended the stairs and grabbed their coats off the hook by the front door.

"What's going on?' Richard called, appearing in the doorway to the study. "You sound like a herd of elephants coming down those stairs." He took a sip from the mug he was holding and leaned against the door frame.

"Sorry, Dad."

He smiled. "Morning girls."

"Hello, Mr Vincent-Payne." her friends chorused.

"We're going to the park to get some air, alright? See you soon." She said brightly, then pushing her friends out of the open front door ahead of her; they hurried out into the cool day, pulling gloves on their hands and woolly hats over their heads.

On the way back from walking Hope home, she told Hannah some of the details of her dream within the dream and of her wish to work together to produce the most awesome paintings in the history of the most awesome paintings ever.

"When I get back from Saint Lucia, we should seriously think about how we're gonna do this."

"Do what, Sal? You haven't told me anything yet." Hannah grinned as she kicked up a few stray leaves on the path they were walking on.

"Sorry, it's just that I need you in on this because I can't do it without you." She said in a tone that caused Hannah's smile to fade slowly and her eyes to widen expectantly. "Smudge, as of today, we're on a mission. Possibly the most important mission of our lives."

"Oh yeah? What a dramatic, intriguing way to get me interested. I'm hooked already." She chuckled. "Let's get back to yours so you can fill me in properly."

Back at the house, she continued ...

"I want us to create an exhibition. Obviously, I am not an artist, so that is where you come in."

"What kind of exhibition?"

"If I could describe the scenes to you well enough, you might be able to paint my visions onto canvas. Not might. I know you can do it."

"Yeah, most probably, but why's it so important? Will they be of interest to other people or just us?" She asked, pushing her glasses up on the bridge of her nose.

"Of interest to everyone." She said immediately. Then she shook her head, offering a half-shrug. "I can't explain it. But I know it will all make sense once we finish the first painting."

"Hmm ..." Hannah considered.

"After that, you can decide whether you're with me all the way or ..."

"All the way where?"

"To the end of ... well, there might be as many as twelve paintings altogether. They might really test your skills, but I've seen what you can do, Smudge. Only you can do this with me. It feels like a sign or something."

"A sign about what?"

"About ... I don't know. Something so good it will somehow help to heal the world ... or something." She finished vaguely.

With the proper support and in partnership with Hannah, she would spend the next few years learning how to manage an exhibition. She would be honing and using her unique skills productively. Then, by the time she was sixteen, she would know how to take advantage of her assets. Inwardly, she sighed with pleasure at how decisive she was being.

"Sounds challenging and beyond radical. I am definitely in." She linked her arm through Sally's. "I've been looking for a special project to focus my art on for the club. Something themed and long-lasting. This could be it, Bubbs."

"Really? You're not just saying that?"

"No. Why would I?"

"Well, it is a bit of a strange request and a big commitment."

"Yeah, I know. It sounds like you have finally found something to dedicate yourself to. It's exciting, and I definitely want to be involved." She squeezed their linked arms tighter. "You'll have to practice your descriptive abilities, though. I mean, obviously, you're quite good at that already, or I couldn't have drawn what you dreamed. When you're in Saint Lucia, you can practice describing the scenes around you there to me when we WhatsApp, so I can imagine it and draw it."

"That's a great idea. Let me try from memory quickly to see what you make of my descriptive abilities."

"Alright. Go on ..."

"Alright. Um. Imagine being in a place that is always warm, with the sun shining from above the clouds, even when it rains. The island has tons of healthy, lush greenery covering all the hills, mountains, and fields, as well as the floors of steep valleys. Everywhere I look, I see green trees of all kinds, fruit trees, and flowers, with sweet smells and fragrances. Smells so good and non-existent in England unless you're actually in a park or something."

"Mmm, I can almost imagine it." She had a faraway look in her eyes.

"Driving on winding, hairpin turn roads gives great views of the sea and is so much fun as you get to see all the pretty, brightly painted homes built higgledy-piggledy in each little town and village. Also, if we are lucky, in Soufriere, one of Andrew's uncles takes us for a ride from one bay to the next in a speed boat. Not in just any old speed boat, but a big, respectfully robust speed boat, because he works for the water police. No, not water police," she corrected, "the marine police or something like that."

"Although I've heard a lot of that before, it always sounds amazing," Hannah said. Sally heard the enthusiasm in her tone and was glad she was inspired. When she left Sally's an hour later, she was excited and eager to begin their mission.

***

That night, as she lay in bed, she thought about the strange, totally awesome place she had visited in the dream, again. She had always thought there was nowhere else in the world she would love better than Saint Lucia. But having experienced the Realm of the Empress in her dream within her dream, she could not forget the sense of peace and harmony, the joy she felt, the light lifting of her heart to heights she never dreamed possible, and a strong sense of it being a place of magical and spiritual unity, beauty, and love. She knew it was not a place she could physically travel to in the usual sense, but one she would have to use her imagination to get to. In this way, with Hannah's help, she could bring the energy of this special place to all.

And in that last moment, just before sleep took her into the depths of her dreams, suddenly, it occurred to her that this was it. This was the ambitious idea she had been searching for. The thing she could work towards. An accomplishment she could be proud of. A dream that was already beginning to swell her heart with anticipation, excitement, and a tiny bit of fear. Fear? Yes. Fear. Because this was a challenge after all. Due to the nature of it, the scope of work involved, and the long-term possibilities, possibly the most difficult in her life. But she was good at facing difficult challenges. She had proved that in the game. Now, she could prove it in real life.

Since playing the game of snakes and ladders, a shift had occurred inside her, and a new force of energy seemed to be fuelling her senses. She was suddenly looking at life and herself differently. It was almost as if it were through a lens that revealed the hidden aspects of human nature to her. She knew that an understanding of this new skill would develop and become more focused over time.

Meanwhile, in the magical Realm of the Empress...

The Timekeeper and the Alchemist were in the cavernous Cradle, discussing the ongoing journey of the young girls. The ever-present sound of rushing water offered a calming backdrop to their conversation. *(T01)*

In the human physical realm...

Lavender Valley, Saint Lucia. March 7th 2020.

Fortunately, or unfortunately, due to the COVID-19 situation, it would be a year before Sally returned to England. She and Hannah begin the first of their extraordinary paintings when she does. Whilst in Saint Lucia, she had talked of her dream of the strange realm with Luke, lead singer of the successful band Deep Silver Lining, and his wife, Sallie.

"It sounds like a beautiful place." She commented, then chuckled softly. "One that, quite strangely, reminds me of something similar that I dreamed of ... This was many years ago."

"We'd be happy to offer some guidance, Rich. You'll need help to get started, right up until they've finished all twelve paintings." Luke said. It was mid-morning, and they were around the pool drinking smoothies. "We can do for them what our parents did for us, can't we, babe? Once we've seen the first painting and understand the talent we're dealing with, we can discuss it all in more detail on a professional level."

"That's a great idea, Luke. I mean, we wouldn't know where to begin with this sort of responsibility, would we, hun?" he called to Simone, who was in the pool.

Having been swimming lengths for the best part of an hour, she gasped her response, "Sounds like a plan ... they'll be in good hands ..."

"Plus, as I said, maybe DSL can sponsor them under a contract. Providing the paintings are good, and the artist is as on board as you are, Sally ..."

"She already is. It's a shame I'm stuck here just when I want to get started." She added a little balefully. Then she checked herself, unable to believe she wanted to be back in England when she was in Saint Lucia, her now second favourite place in the world, having been moved off its first-place position by the Realm of the Empress.

"Best to see this as an opportunity to plan what you'll need to do when you get back. Use this time constructively, and keep Hannah up to speed with your thoughts and arrangements." Luke advised her.

As a child genius who had formed a band with his schoolmates in their early teens, Luke understood well the long-term commitment, passion, and determination required to succeed. However, he could see the same passion he possessed in Sally, and since she and Hannah were children of his good friends from way back when, it was good to see the next generation passionate about working selflessly and creatively to bring hope to the world, just as he had over the years with his music.

"As I said, once we've seen the first painting, we'll know just how much talent we're dealing with."

"Hannah is in one hundred per cent and the most gifted artist I've ever known. Not that I know many," she chuckled.

"Alright, first things first. Where would she like to paint if not at home?"

"They could use the house." Sallie suggested, "I mean, if we're going to spend more time here, it could be perfect. We can reorganise the two rooms on the ground floor, and it will be good knowing someone is in the house during our absence. They can work there on weekends, and the housekeeper or their parents can keep an eye on them." Sally's mind was buzzing as her eyes lit up. She had been to their house a few times before. They had a swimming pool, a sauna, a gym, and everything. Which meant Hope could come to swim and work out while Hannah painted. "We can easily arrange for them to be picked up, brought to the house on Saturday mornings, and then dropped home that evening or even on Sundays. And, of course, you'd be welcome to go there too, although, as I said, the housekeeper will be there."

"That's so generous of you," Simone said as she sat on the steps in the water.

"I know what it's like to be passionate about an idea and totally focused on achieving it when you're so young. They will need the right support around them," said Luke.

As the adults continued discussing the possible arrangements to support Sally in her new endeavour, she went searching for Andrew. She found him in the kitchen taking a long drink from a bottle of pineapple Turbo. Before she left a few weeks back, he had hugged her close, declared that he loved her and asked if she would be his girlfriend.

"We're as close as my mum and dad were." He said, "I know we'll only get to see each other in the summer, but ... I love you and ..." He looked at her anxiously.

"Drew ..." she interrupted, deciding to relieve him of his uncertainty around how she might respond. "It's alright; I want to be your girlfriend." She shrugged casually, then impulsively kissed his cheek. "I love you too."

Since playing the game, Sally somehow felt – older. She was seeing Andrew differently too. At fourteen and a half, he was already his father's son. His interest in carpentry was solid, and his skills were growing. He was too young to use any of the complicated, sharper tools or machinery, but he was learning about the different types of wood, carving, cutting directions, and joinery. When not in school, he attended meetings with potential clients and suppliers with his dad. He would learn the business from the ground up and it take over one day. He was the spitting image of his dad at the same age and already taller than average. He was also his mother's son, however, for he was interested in fitness, enjoyed yoga, was respectful of nature and had a sentimental, soft side when it came to her.

His skinny chest puffed out as he took a slow, deep breath in relief. His grin was wide and happy. "Cool. cool." He pulled his goggles down over his eyes, shouting. "*Now, the last one in the pool's a green coconut!*" as he ran back outside, with her chasing after him.

During the next four years, Sally and Hannah completed the first painting, titled The Question, and then obtained full backing from Deep Silver Lining to continue. Further paintings were titled The Answer, The Truth, The Revelation, The Third Way, Joy, Acceptance, Life, Love, Togetherness, Completion and Humankind.

A loving, spiritual energy would direct the rest of her life. An energy that respects nature and the natural abundance provided by Mother Earth. As she matures, she shall evolve a great sense of protection towards all living creatures, and her curiosity and consideration for all people shall be important aspects of her life. She shall eventually become a true humanitarian.

9

In the magical Realm of the Empress ...

From the unseen, the Timekeeper, their old wise eyes distant and glowing a silvery hue, watched intently, absolutely absorbed in the task at hand. They continuously manoeuvred their time translation rings with impossible dexterity while reviewing Salliniquai's trial.

Infused with Salliniquai's Empresserial energy, Sally was drawn into a trial of her own where her faith in herself, her instincts, and her intuitions were tested. By standing strong and remembering her reason for needing to win the game, she successfully returned to the real world, and Salliniquai's trial was a success.

Within the amethyst geode of the Elevated One...

On Salliniquai's arrival back into the realm, the Awakener immediately put her into a form of stasis as the flower petals unfolded around her. A partial, conscious awareness of her surroundings remained, ensuring the continual gentle chime of her Empresserial energy and the never-ending wind sent their unique tone across the land. As they were busy receiving attunements in the unseen, the Elevated One had not yet appeared, and Salliniquai was aware of this. She had made it to earth and back within the same sun turn and, whilst congratulating herself, decided to make a second jump. The jewelled symbol of Venus had reappeared upon her forehead, and she immediately began to converse with the Awakener telepathically.

"So, as you have witnessed, I am more than capable of channelling my energy appropriately." Her green eyes, behind her closed lids, were sparkling with life and excitement as she expressed her thoughts and feelings about her adventure, then added, "Although the experience was not quite what I expected." She sent them an impression of a sour look. "I suspect you intended to try to dissuade me from going again by sending me for a trial within those childish circumstances?"

"The Empress sees the truth of all. Indeed, you did so prove yourself, Empress." replied the Awakener. "One is more than worthy of a full life in the earthly realm."

"Oh, be still." She snapped while her senses reached out for any sign of the Elevated One. "Time is of the essence. I'm ready to be sent through to experience a full human life as a woman."

The Awakener's gasp was not in the least bit subtle. "But Empress, we do not have the capacity to ensure the ..."

"What aspect of your capacity is missing?" She interrupted rudely. The Awakener imagined the sharp query would be accompanied by a deep sigh of impatience, with hands resting on her hips, had she been awake because, unfortunately, she had the somewhat spoilt, haughty, self-important attitude of a potential ruler not yet evolved enough to be wise to certain manners and courtesies, shall we say.

Trying to stall, the Awakener replied, "You have much to learn before the Offering, Empress. Time is of the essence, and the difficulty is we cannot call forth the Jump to ..."

She interrupted them. "It is fortunate then that as my years are young, I shall be flower-petalled in this instance. My lifeline shall remain connected if I am flower-petalled, will it not? As it did so during my trial. My time within the human physical realm will most likely be as short as this, regardless of how long my life is on the earth. I shall remain bound to this place and return to this spot as long as a petal remains." Using powers unmatched by any other, she thought of the spell required, and carefully detaching one of the large petals, laid it down outside the circle of brown earth. She conveyed the relevant words in high Malsimily, then confirmed confidently, still in thought. "I shall return in no time at all."

The Awakener agreed reluctantly. "As you say."

"Yes. As *I say*." She threw back, her tone decidedly snippy. Again, the Awakener could imagine her furtively looking around for any sign of the Elevated One. The Awakener made no move or action to progress her request but stated hesitantly,

"There is a further difficulty ..."

Even telepathically, she could not hide her irritation. "Which is?"

"Why, the Malsimily elements required to support your journey to the earth, which holds the four aspects of the soul together, retaining the unification of the Trilogy Empress. For should they separate ..."

"That is why *you* are here, to ensure a separation does *not* happen."

"We shall do our best, Empress." Reciting a series of magical incantations, the Awakener infused the studded, jewelled symbol of the feminine, which became invisible.

Quite pleased with herself now, Salliniquai assumed she had gotten her own way and was going back to the human physical realm. She reined in her arrogant tone, remembering they were only looking out for her as was their duty.

"You must not fear for me, Awakener." She sighed gently. "I shall be back before you know it, before the Elevated One knows it and well before too many turns of the sun have passed. I have no intention of jeopardising my charge."

She added this last statement to appease us, the Awakener thought, noticing the mischievous tone in her telepathy. It troubled them.

"As you say, Empress."

"Yes, as I say. Now, open it again and do not fret so. There is a strong link between us. Yes, the Elevated One might be expressly, um, astonished by my absence, but they shall remain loyal to my efforts. I am not worried. As you should not be." She thought, sending them a vision of herself, dismissively flapping her hand.

"Astonished is not the word we would use to describe the possible wrath of the Elevated One," murmured the Awakener, pressing their hand to their precious Venus amulet, hanging from the chocker around their neck. By speaking out loud, the Empress would not have heard their comment.

Salliniquai, meanwhile, was busy secretly casting a spell upon the separated petal outside the circle of the earth. At her unspoken command, the petal disintegrated but left a reflection of itself in the seen to fool the Awakener. Inside the flower bud, she sunk deeper into its soft, fluffy centre as the large purple petals closed around her. She was excited to be beginning her next adventure. To live the life of a human woman was indeed the one thing she so desperately desired because she wished to know the love of a human man.

The never-ending wind gradually died down to a mere whisper as she thought the mantra in the language of the Malsimily, which, along with the Awakener's ministrations, would help draw her back to the earth. Beginning her second journey as the flower portal opened beneath her, she relaxed into the sense of weightlessness and dropped down through the stem.

At last! She was on her way to the earth again, and nothing could reverse it. She frowned at a sudden, unfamiliar shifting sensation *Oh!? Something is happening ... This was not how it felt when she ...* All at once, her Empresserial energies were frozen, and a pale-yellow glow surrounded her form within the flower. The life she so wished to experience was, unfortunately or fortunately, destined to be more complex than she expected. Whatever was happening, she would activate the censoring charm, then link it to the Awakener, she decided. This way, they will know it was she who initiated this. The magic might affect them unusually somehow, but it was her earthly life they were talking about here. She would do anything for a chance to live it.

The process to progress her next jump through the purple flower portal, which had yet to be authorised, had been pre-emptively initiated by the Awakener. Fortunately, the Elevated One shimmered into the seen moments later and, with one sweeping glance, knew something was wrong with the current situation. They moved up beside the Awakener.

"Vek Paidus Kay Conarium-Ella." (What is going on here?) they asked immediately, as their orb retracted back into the unseen. "Dimsulu Empress Salliniquai?" (What has happened to the Empress Salliniquai?)

"We initialised the single sun turn sleep to ensure when she incarnates again, it shall be within a mature woman, O Elevated One," replied the Awakener, chuckling softly. "She wanted to revisit the human physical realm right away, and we could not refuse. To do that, we had to initialise her jump."

Upon the raised dais, the Elevated One immediately began preparations to take control of the situation. Standing with their back turned towards the geode's open side, they magically brought one of several altars, a sturdy altar of dark, knobbly wood covered with pots, jars, bowls, and other items with magical properties, into the seen. While gesturing and weaving their hands deliberately, the Elevated One turned to their androgynous companion.

"Her progression has been stayed for a time," they observed in a soft tone, purposely avoiding eye contact with the Awakener. It grated that they had not been present to prepare the Empress when this was their allocated training time with her. To make doubly sure the endeavour was successful, they would make the appropriate changes with their deliberate, spell-guiding hands and supreme, magical abilities, with the support of the Timekeeper, which would safeguard Salliniquai to some degree. "Whilst she remains in the single sun turn sleep, we must move quickly to align the time element." They announced, their purposeful gestures swift and their tone efficient, as they brought another of their altars, made purely of white, smoky light, into the seen. "Timekeeper, attend me." They called softly.

Immediately, the Timekeeper's tall, scholarly figure shimmered into view to hover close to the Elevated One. Raising their heavily ringed hands, they pushed back the hood of their robe, revealing old, wise eyes and narrow, expressionless features. They spoke in their usual hushed monotone as one hand continually worked the set of time translation rings on each finger. They bowed in greeting.

"We are here, O Elevated One. At the request of the Alchemist, we reviewed her trial upon the earth and saw into the future of the young human host, which is now in full possession of the Hereditary Kee. The timeline is currently right for the Empress to begin working through all four of her lessons, beginning with the lesson on trauma."

The Elevated One acknowledged their appearance with a slight bow of their head. "Alright. We can begin the transitional awakening process and ensure the nine Malsimily elements are infused ..."

The Awakener swallowed deeply, *"Nine* Malsimily elements?"

The Elevated One paused their hand-weaving actions and turned their measured gaze to the Awakener.

"There are nine Malsimily elements *vital* to her time spent in the human physical realm, yes. By infusing the energy of these elements into objects and people, they provide her with guidance, protection, and safety. The Timekeeper manages three of those elements through magical time manipulation while we infuse the other six in varying degrees. Which of these did you infuse?"

The Awakener, though caught off guard, offered a partial, positive response to the question. "Crystals. We infused her Venus symbol."

"She shall retain her natural draw to crystals as a supportive energy then. Chakra crystals in particular."

The Awakeners clasped their hands together before them,

smiling slightly. "Then all is in hand for us to ..."

"No, wait a moment!" The Elevated One interrupted, pausing to assess the charged energy they could sense around the Empress. "O my Empress. Her energy is ... separating ... into four energy streams!"

Within the flower petals, meanwhile, Salliniquai's eyes flew open, and she gasped in surprise. She could feel a separation occurring but could not act on what she realised was happening.

"... Her trinity of life has divided into four." The Elevated One gasped in shock. "She is to live through four incarnations upon the earth, and ... yes, one of her incarnations is destined to evolve in the human physical realm but shall be drawn to the Land of Ludonia. The other three shall stay in the human physical realm. Awakener, fetch the remaining four Knights of the Brotherhood of the Nine at once! They must follow her into the same span of linear time. Go, now." Although abruptly spoken, their tone was soft.

The Awakener's golden orb appeared into the seen as a flat disk, expanded into a glowing orb around them, and then shimmered away with them inside.

"Timekeeper, attend me." The Timekeeper hovered forward once again. "First, we shall disperse the familial bond. Without the Hereditary Kee, the bond will create extreme emotional difficulties. To make up for this, we will create realm bonds to pair the knights and the incarnations with each other. The attraction can then evolve naturally between them. Secondly, the links to ensure the rest of the elements are appropriately infused will require construction." The Elevated One announced. "Infusing the staff is the only way to ensure all nine elements are present when they travel through the jump." Instantly, a small, emerald green orb the size of a grapefruit appeared, hovering above their open palm. They spoke the words with the Timekeeper gripping the staff with one hand while working their time translation magic with the other. Closing their eyes briefly, the Elevated One softly sang the spell's words.

"Empress Salliniquai, now upon the earth, live a human life from six, not birth.

They began to weave and gesture elegantly, automatically making light patterns in the air with the orb.

No child shall you bear of your own; with parents gone, you will be alone.

The orb was set to rest upon the crown-shaped head of the staff.

No host will know their family's past; a search for parents is a hope not cast.

The orb melted and began to infuse its glow into the staff.

When the time arises, you shall awaken, and the good knights' triggers shall transform and open.

Sinuously, in glowing, swirling patterns, the magic weaved its way down the shaft.

Sent in your wake so all shall understand, your true destinies are within this land ..."

Releasing the staff, which stayed upright and fixed in place, the Elevated One turned back to the altar, exhaling a relieved sigh.

"There. It is done. Now, in the way of the Malsimily, the lesser kees relate to her four lessons, the jump preparation, and the creation of the cradles. For all to succeed, we must work within the same leap year used in her trial. The year 2020. Fortunately, the time factor is more easily manipulated in a leap year, correct?"

"That is so," confirmed the Timekeeper.

"Exceptional. We shall come to that in a moment ..." Suddenly, they sensed that a tiny segment in their timeline had been disturbed. However, the desire to pursue the disruption was not there, for knowing the Timekeeper had seen fit to intervene was reassuring. Within a few minutes, the Awakener orbed back into the seen and approached the Elevated One.

"We have the knights, O Elevated One." They offered the box containing the four remaining knights of the Brotherhood of the Nine. Within the box were nine circular receptacles in three rows of three. Five were empty. Four items, resembling the large mango fruit seeds, sat within the remaining receptacles. Each had a lock of hair growing out from the centre of the seed. One was a spray of red; the second was hair of a deep honey colour; the third was almost white; and the last was black. The Timekeeper turned to address the Elevated One.

"Her trial was completed successfully. There were equal influences the Empress had to deal with from the hidden realm of magical dreams and the human physical realm."

The Elevated One glanced briefly at the Awakener. "According to the Awakener, that is so. We cannot imagine why you believed that risking our Empress ..."

"O Elevated One, we never thought for a moment we were anywhere near capable of ..." Their sudden, uncharacteristic chortle interrupted their explanation. "...of successfully carrying out the task, but all was in alignment. We could not delay once the Empress ..."

The Elevated One almost scoffed with grudging admiration. "She put a spell on you to believe it was so, as well as ..."

The Awakener's mouth dropped open in astonishment. "She put a spell on us, why the little ...," they giggled again. "It was our understanding that making the transition during the conclusion of her sleeping spell of rest was necessary."

"That is true as a re-energising, meditative sleep, yes, but not as a way to avoid my ministrations," replied the Elevated One.

Although the situation was serious, the Awakener chuckled again. "The requirement for four incarnations instead of simply one is quite complex ..."

"Having had no influence over her energy during the transition ..." the Elevated One interrupted with an edge to their voice, directing a brief look of reproach toward the Awakener, "...the four incarnations have arisen because the energy of the Empress is far too potent to be hosted by one single human without our help expanding the Hereditary Kee. Which we assume was necessary during her trial?"

"That is correct, O Elevated One. As the first human to host the energy of the Empress in her true, complete form, the Empresserial energy shall remain with young Sally. Their glorious, spiritual connection shall be as permanent and binding as it is hereditary." The Awakener practically sang.

Ignoring the Awakener's hearty manner, the Elevated One drew out a puff of black smoke from a coil-shaped yellow bar, which then expanded around them. They continued.

"In that case, one lesser Kee shall be bound to each incarnation. In terms of the Sallee incarnation, when she and the knight come of age in the human physical realm, they shall be drawn to Ludonia, while the other three remain in the human physical realm."

"The social situations and life experiences of her four incarnations shall be quite diverse, will they not?" the Timekeeper queried. Although they already knew the answers to all they asked.

"It is as you say, Timekeeper," replied the Elevated One.

"And her protection against the Book of Stone?" they queried again, seeking confirmation of what they already knew would come to pass.

"The Book of Stone? Yes. Her Empresserial energy shall guide her in this. In terms of her welfare during her lives, with a knight of the Brotherhood of the Nine being duly charged and charmed with various elements of the charm spell, they shall carry out their duty as her rescuer and protector with high honour and unwavering valour."

"Except for that one life, where more of my ministrations were necessary." The Timekeeper added cryptically, turning away slightly. "Notwithstanding the usual translations, a requirement for interference occurs twice for the Sallee incarnation in Ludonia. The thought dispersal spell does not work on the Green Oracle; therefore, a more direct approach shall be necessary at the appropriate time. We can easily interrupt the time stream. It will be sorted, trust me."

The Elevated One gave them a long, considering look. *Sorted?* But chose to ignore the strange reference. "And in the other incarnated lives?"

"Around nine times for the Sallyanne incarnation. The others require no interference of major significance."

When it became clear the Timekeeper had nothing further to add, the Awakener spoke, their smile overly bright and wide, their words jovial.

"Then we have prepared well."

"This is no laughing matter, Awakener. We must remember these impromptu lives shall not be without difficulty. Although she merely embraces the human experience through hosts, her incarnations will have to deal with risky, dangerous situations and corruptible people to ensure her four lessons are learned fully," said the Elevated One, their tone serious.

"Ahh, so by making certain the love which evolves between each Empress and a knight is of a spiritual, twin flame quality, their bonds shall be unbreakable," observed the Timekeeper. "You understand the thoughts and passions of human men well, O Elevated One."

"That is so. It is the reason why we made the charm so potent. As one of the nine Malsimily elements, they shall immediately respond to it, consciously or not."

"On the spiritual level first?"

The Elevated One nodded once, slowly. "This element shall ensure the similar energy of the two is immediately recognisable on the spiritual level. They will be bonded naturally in ways not immediately apparent at their first meeting, and the knights shall be drawn to their Salliniquai incarnations as strongly as they will be to them because of their charge of retaining the kurren-see." A sprinkle of multicoloured, star-shaped flashes exploded around them, glittering brightly, then winking out. "Also, as all are from the Realm of the Empress, there is a strong possibility of language similarities occurring when expressing their thoughts, feelings, and love. There will always be a natural sense of reverence for one another, as well as a mutual respect."

"Precisely." Chuckled the Awakener. "For what is the human experience if all aspects of life are not a part of it? That is, apart from the familial blood bond of parent and child, which shall be taken from her somehow." Their eyes were downcast, and their expression was one of sorrow.

"Yes, yes, that is unfortunate and indeed a sad situation, but there was no choice." The Elevated One gestured impatiently whilst glancing over at the Awakener, a sharp look in their eyes. "Any desire to search for earthly parents or investigate the lineage or roots of her family had to be quelled. Going down that road would only lead to confusion, disappointment, and possibly further complications. She will sense it is better to leave that part of her life alone. Letting it remain a mystery."

"It pleases us to know the knight shall arrive in her life when she needs him most. At a time when she may feel alone, vulnerable even," the Awakener said brightly, smiling widely again.

Ignoring their happy face, the Elevated One replied. "It pleases us, too. They shall (True Malsimily, translation unavailable) especially when they meet."

"Then we only need to ensure all eight energies are protected from the Great Suffering, the worst threat of all, O Elevated One." The Timekeeper murmured meaningfully, "as well as avoiding being tainted with the subsequent man-made vaccines."

"That consideration is in the hands of two of our charges Timekeeper. Providing all eight energies make it through, Salliniquai will have the stone harvest to stay on her return, and just four sun turns remaining to get to the Distance for the Offering."

Hovering back slightly, the Timekeeper shook their head regretfully. "Hmm, we do so wish we could offer assurances, but as you know, we cannot do so. The knowledge of such things and being unable to speak of them is quite a pain in the bum, actually."

The Elevated One, busy weaving and gesticulating as they continued to organise the unique spells for the four knights, frowned curiously at the Timekeeper's unusual articulation and display of speech in the earthly language. They were usually so enigmatic in their expressions. The Elevated One questioned their new-found form of expression.

"We are curious as to why you speak so, Timekeeper. You have been using unfamiliar language we do not understand which does not possess the eloquence of the realm. For example, you said earlier *kicks off*, *mad coincidence*, and just now, *pain in the bum?* Your linguistic ability is becoming ..." To the surprise of the Elevated One and the Awakener, the Timekeeper, for perhaps one of the first times ever, grinned broadly, and almost chuckled.

"We are simply preparing for the return of the Empress. She will have changed much during her years within the human physical realm and will be well-versed in the earthly language. We are merely ..." They paused, quite dramatically, the Awakener thought, "familiarising ourselves with the earthly references and slang. Since the human element shall be a part of her, or perhaps more accurately, since love has been established through her lives as human women, the Empress will be a tad more ... chilled out." The Awakener glanced at the Timekeeper again, almost desperate to know more but unwilling to risk further reproach from the Elevated One.

"As you say, Timekeeper. We recognise there must be a purpose to this from your understanding of the situation." The Elevated One said mildly. "Would you advise creating a fictional place where the incarnations and the knights can all gravitate towards? It would absolutely ensure a grounded energetic link so they may find the incarnations."

The Timekeeper's features settled into their usual expression of calm objectivity once more as they stated mildly, "It is done, O Elevated One."

"Oh?" The steady gaze of the Elevated One held the Timekeeper's for a long moment.

"For young Sally initially, for Salliniquai's trial." They explained. "We created a safe place because we cannot control the element of free will in the actions and behaviours of all involved."

"Ahh," they nodded sagely, "can we look into her lives without displacing the timeline?"

The Timekeeper hovered closer. "This is possible. As the Empresserial seed, it is young Sally's generation who shall introduce the world to the Third Way after the war."

Each laid a hand upon the Elevated One's staff. The two then spent long moments gazing intensely at the staff just below the symbol of Venus. In their minds, they saw what would pass in the life of Sally.

"All of their fates have been reviewed and shall develop as expected during their lives." The Timekeeper said once they released the staff and hovered back a little. "The place we created to keep the knights and the incarnations safe is called Rowanshire." There was an unusual hint of pride in their voice.

"Exceptional. Then, if all goes well, the energies of her incarnations and the knights of the Brotherhood of the Nine shall return to the Realm of the Empress at the appointed time."

The Timekeeper nodded once, slowly. "Exactly." They turned away slightly. "Observing how she navigated the human physical realm as the incarnations was interesting. Their lives were quite remarkable, beyond fascinating, and truly revealing of human nature," they added, an uncharacteristic, faraway look in their eyes.

The Awakener glanced at the Timekeeper enviously now. "It shall be most interesting to see the Empress in her separated incarnations upon their return."

The Elevated One sighed wistfully. "Sometimes we wish we were party to all you see, Timekeeper. For now, however, time is of the essence. How are the translations going?"

"Very well. Do not concern yourself. I shall not translate the secret, significant part of the Knowing until the appropriate time."

"We must move quickly to align the time element exactingly in all four of her lives," said the Elevated One. Their purposeful gestures were swift as they brought another of their altars into the seen and murmured a litany of unusual sounds and words. "To ensure her incarnations can settle the lessons within their energetic forms, she shall require a rest period at the closure of her experiences until the appointed jump time approaches. We need your manipulations to ensure this. Attend me, Timekeeper."

Hovering beside them, the Timekeeper assisted by grasping the Elevated One's staff to reinforce the spell's power, while their other hand worked their time translation rings. Then they backed away as the Elevated One turned to the Awakener and asked directly.

"When you transitioned her directly from her sleep to the portal, did she cast a spell to ensure the stone harvest remained dormant in her absence?"

"Spell?"

"Yes, spell. Do not tell me that you ...?" The Elevated One stopped talking momentarily, a distant look of deep assessment appearing in their gaze. A sweet, fruity scent had permeated the air from their ministrations.

The Awakener, believing the Elevated One to be considering a spell, waited patiently for a long moment. Then assuming Elevated One's attention had returned, they asked, "In her divided state, can she retain the memories of all of the incarnations?" Which momentarily distracted the Elevated One from their focus beyond the boundary of the geodes. Seeing that the Elevated One was preoccupied, the Timekeeper spoke,

"That may not be known until her return, Awakener. She will test her spiritual strength through the experience of family dysfunction, societal discriminations and conflicts, and personal trials and tribulations to gain a true understanding of the state of the world that is the human physical realm."

The Elevated One, concerned now with what was happening at the Sierthern boundary, glanced somewhat irritably at the Awakener's inappropriate, Cheshire cat grin.

Meanwhile ...

At the realms most Sierthern boundary at the end of the Sier road, a few minutes after the Empress had been flower petalled for the second time, the single drop of clear as crystal water held within a dark, dry, bottomless well just beyond the south love fields, began to turn grey.

A thin crack appeared on a stone-crusted orb set in a circle of stone beneath the drop of water within the well, and an unusual tremor began beneath it—a tremor with purpose and direction. As the crack started to widen the single drop of water dropped onto it and rolled off, tendrils of misty smoke puffing out as it hissed and fizzed, followed by a trickle of a living, writhing, grey substance. As the outer shell cracked further, a stone fall of molten rock bubbled, frothed, and gushed out.

Growing exponentially, the dark, sticky mass overflowed the edge of the well, covering all in its path with a sludge-like, grey matter. The substance, called the Stone Harvest, was deadly to all life. Now awakened, the intelligent nature of it changed, as did the texture, depending on the surface it was covering. Thickening and transforming into a liquid tar-like substance now, it seeped away in all directions, beginning to cover the land in the Realm of the Empress.

Paralysing all that it touched, the Stone Harvest was an unstoppable, re-making force set to destroy all the nature the Empress had created within the realm. Only the cleansing waters of the Distance could stay and reverse this danger, but for that to occur, the Empress must fulfil her sacrificial duty.

10

Within the amethyst geode of the Elevated One ...

While sending one altar back to the unseen and bringing another into the seen, the Elevated One turned their attention to the Awakener.

"It is too late for recriminations and regrets around your actions, Awakener, for the Stone Harvest is conscious now. We must do all we can to support her endeavours, even as they are going badly wrong."

"Badly wrong, you say?" queried the Awakener

"Yes, wrong," the Elevated One replied crossly. "We must ensure the remaining Malsimily elements are sent through before her arrival." They glanced at the Timekeeper, who nodded affirmatively.

"Precisely, O Elevated One." The Awakener giggled again.

The Elevated One sighed resignedly, shaking their head a little woefully.

"This is why the rules of inter-realm transportation are so strict. There are elements to incarnations which must be adhered to, to ensure a smooth, directed transition from the sleep spell."

"But she commanded us to complete the transition ..." the Awakener countered hastily, in their defence.

"Be that as it may, only *we* have the relevant magical knowledge to be soul-specific with such an earthly bound contract. Only *we* have the sacred knowledge of the Knowing. Only *we* understand that every human life has a higher soul contract to fulfil, which must not be interfered with. We alone have the skill and authority to master this. You do not possess the knowledge to ensure she fulfils the Trilogy and returns ready for the Offering, do you?"

The Awakener's gaze was quite troubled now. "Why no, Elevated One." They stammered.

"What actions did you take to ensure her relationships would be charmed and she would be awakened at the appointed time and brought back?"

The Awakener hesitated, the Elevated One and the Timekeeper were watching them closely, waiting for their response. "The ... actions?" They were becoming less merry and more distressed as the Elevated One pointed out their failures. They could not stop expressing their happiness, however.

"Yes, the actions. Must you continually throw our own questions back at us?" the Elevated One demanded, their tone, quite uncharacteristically, was laced with anger and scorn. The Awakener seemed to have no idea how serious the situation was, or how irritating their continued happy countenance was.

The Awakener flinched, taking a small step back at the rebuke. "We were not aware ..." they stammered again, "we are deeply sorry, O Elevated One. Have we truly jeopardised the ...?"

The Elevated One interrupted them. "If truth be told (*True Malsimily. Translation unavailable*)." Seeing that the Awakener's shoulders had drooped, their frustration dissipated a little, recognising that they were not conducting themselves in the spiritual vibration of the Realm of the Empress, but who could blame them? It was not a situation they were expecting to have to deal with. They took a deep, calming breath.

"It is not entirely your fault, Awakener, as one must, of course, do as one sees fit at the time or as one is commanded," they conceded in a gentler tone. "Fear not. As long as we act immediately to ensure her safety and prepare for her return using a trigger, all shall be well." Behind the look of reassurance shown to the Awakener, however, deep within them, a sense of apprehension had begun to grow. Without the Empress herself being present in the realm, the two sound constants keeping the Stone Harvest at bay were no longer present. The Stone Harvest had already begun its creepy progression, and to them, the silence within the realm was deafening.

"Now, back to the locations and the jump dates for the two portals. One is to be in the Land of Ludonia, the other in the human physical realm." They turned to the Awakener. "How long was it before she returned from her trial?"

"Mere moments, O Elevated One. A minute or two, perhaps."

The Timekeeper spoke up. "It was nine minutes exactly, and we have already seen to this aspect, O Elevated One."

"Excellacious. It occurred within the cycle of nine then, allowing the time factor to be more easily manipulated in a leap year. This is good for the jump date the six energies in the human physical realm must jump on."

"And the jump date for the two energies at the second portal in Ludonia?" The Awakener asked.

The Timekeeper responded. "As time works differently in this realm, it requires no significant interference. Our timekeeping was required on two occasions only. The one we spoke of earlier was a minor adjustment to their timeline when they were in separate realms, and the other ..." They let the sentence hang. "Both were in company with the Green Oracle. Be assured we have seen to all timely re-interactions."

"Precisely. Understood," chuckled the Awakener.

With their powers joined through the staff, the Timekeeper and the Elevated One could see ahead of time into the Empresses' lives.

"Reveal the faces of the incarnations, Timekeeper." The Elevated One said. "We wish to see the women the Empresserial energy naturally selected."

With a slight flick of their nifty fingers, a small, glittering green orb appeared. "This is Empress Sallee, for which we have set the Hive portal." A layer of the orb dematerialised, revealing the heart-shaped face of an Indian girl. Then, it thickened again. "For Empress Sallie, Empress Sallyanne, and Empress Sallori in the human physical realm, we have set the Island portal," A layer of the orb dematerialised again, revealing one after the other, a young, west Indian woman, with a bright smile. An Afro-Caribbean woman with a scarred face. Then, the face of Sallori, a British woman with olive skin and rosy cheeks. All had green eyes and dimples when they smiled. The orb disappeared with a flick of the Timekeeper's finger.

"On which island was the portal placed?" asked the Awakener.

"Following our observations, there were three least affected by the Great Suffering during its first four variants."

The Elevated One paused. "Your recommendation?"

"May we come to that later? The chosen island has a relatively small population of primarily Nubian folk, a jewel of nature in many respects as well as being young regarding its spiritual development."

The Elevated One murmured an incantation in High Malsimily. With a precise weaving of their hands, two sparks of light appeared and hovered just above and before them.

"Timekeeper. Which of the earthly solstices is more potent, the winter or summer?"

"The summer solstice is the most potent, O Elevated One."

The Elevated One murmured more words in High Malsimily, then said, "The Kees are now fully infused. On the day of the summer solstice in the leap year of 2020, the way shall open from the first dark twelfth hour to the second light twelfth hour of that day on the island chosen. A twelve-earth-hour window in which they can all make the jump. Now, we must send the knights through to complete their lessons with her while you travel to the Alchemist's cradle, Awakener." The Elevated One began to instruct the Awakener as to how to proceed.

***

A note from the Timekeeper ...

As the Elevated One directs the Awakener, we can reveal some valuable information that has been translated with a degree of caution. Too much of this knowledge all at once can cause irreparable damage to the human mind, and as we are of a purely spiritual nature, we absolutely reject the idea of willingly risking this harm to another. As such, not all concerning Salliniquai's onward journey shall be revealed here.

Historically, the events within the human physical realm that led to the time of the Great Suffering were no accident. They were a long time in the making. These conditions have occurred during the outgoing Piscean age, while the masculine element has guided the development of the earth. Unfortunately, as the masculine has for many, many, *many* long years sought to destroy the truth of the feminine, as well as lessen her powerful energy in every way, shape and form, such guidance, and the selfish, self-obsessed steering of humanity towards solely masculine drives and desires, has been hugely detrimental to the world at large.

One only needs to investigate how the evolving nature of the feminine element was damaged, demeaned, dismissed, and almost destroyed by the masculine throughout the earth's history, to understand the nature and the repercussions of such actions.

In their defence, as well as to show we are not simply discriminating against all human males in general, those touched by the energy of the nine kings cannot go against their natures. Men thrive in a capitalist society and, from a position of strength, take advantage of women, people of colour, and the most vulnerable. This led to returning karma steeped in the emperor's energy. It is a cycle that must be broken down if humankind is to survive.

As to the Empress Salliniquai. Stubbornly wilful and as impatient as ever to learn her lessons of love, she was shown how life unfolds upon the earth in her lessons with the Timekeeper (*who is not to be blamed for her short-sighted, petulant actions, which have landed us all in it by the way*). After those sneak peeks, she restlessly began to desire a life on earth as a human woman. Rather than wait for the appointed time to visit the human physical realm, our impulsive and somewhat unlearned young Empress bit off more than she could chew, got more than she bargained for, and dropped herself right in it when her energy divided, causing her to live four separate lives upon the earth instead. (*As you can see, we are getting the gist of the earthly slang terms better than ever*).

Within the amethyst geode of the Elevated One ...

"Awakener, working with the energy of the Empress, is not merely about saying the words and drawing the symbols. Power must be drawn from the realm and the Empress herself," the Elevated One explained patiently. "She knew what she was doing, trusting you to send her through this way. She could have commanded the Alchemist to send her through or the Timekeeper. But she chose you and this portal specifically while we were busy." The Awakener's expression changed, and their shade brightened a little at the thought of being specially chosen by the Empress. "She also chose this portal because she knew that should anything go wrong, we would be right here surrounded by everything required to ensure her safe existence in that realm, as well as her timely return." They turned to the Awakener. "Time is of the essence. Come." Now they had a moment to spare; with a few words spoken in High Malsimily, the Elevated One removed the spell Salliniquai had cast upon the Awakener. "You must make haste to the Alchemist."

"As you say, O Elevated One." At their silent command, the Awakener's orb appeared from the unseen. "For the love of Empress Salliniquai." They said, clasping their hands together.

The Elevated One and the Timekeeper mirrored the action responding in kind, "For the love of Empress Salliniquai."

Encased within their orb, the Awakener floated to the travel well, sinking inside and out of sight.

Once the two were alone, the Elevated One turned to the Timekeeper. "We shall infuse four earth Angels tasked to guide the Empresses until the knight's arrival."

"May we know who you chose to magically enchant?"

"Yes. All four were chosen for their spiritual maturity because if they met only once or were around for years, their energy would calm and support her. The nature of the relationship depends upon how humanly evolved she is destined to become within each life."

"That sounds sufficiently satisfactory." The Timekeeper stood watching the Elevated One as they picked up a strange, knobbly object, pressed their lips to it and blew. Deep and alluring, flute-like notes enriched the air materialising as a stream of light that formed into a large droplet of realm waters. After echoing for an impossibly long time, the sound died away as that part of the magic was completed and held in place until it was cast into the jump.

"As each knight is sent through to a particular life stream, we shall set the Empresserial trigger via the charmed books, bring forth the Angels, and commit the Kees in the form of a drop of realm water added just before the portal closes. It will send the energy of one Angel and one triple-layered Kee as a spark to each fork of the Empress's life streams." The Timekeeper nodded approvingly.

"What about her situations and experiences during these four lives. They will be quite different, will they not?"

"It is as you say, Timekeeper." They paused, glancing briefly at them, "Wait a moment. The first split approaches." The Elevated One turned back to the altar. Carefully lifting the first seed from the box, they placed it upon the circle of brown earth and murmured the incantation that brought the knight shimmering up into a full-grown being held in stasis. The charge, some of which was in High Malsimily, was telepathically communicated and infused into the knight. Once the ritual was complete, they explained further.

"There shall be similarities in her lives and the sort of earthly personality she evolves. For example, in all her lives, she will feel a deep emptiness at some point. She will be inclined to search for the unknown element she feels is missing from her life."

"A true love?"

"A true, *spiritual* love. She will be naturally spiritual, of course, for she is, in truth, an ethereal being. It shall be almost impossible to corrupt her true nature or knock her off each fateful life path."

"Almost?"

The Elevated One sighed. "Nothing is infallible."

The Timekeeper conceded a slight nod, then said cautiously,

"On earth, there shall be many risks and threats to her survival."

Beneath their veil, the Elevated One's benevolent expression changed to one of pride. "We have faith in Salliniquai being able to defeat such elements." Having infused the charge to the knight, the Elevated One called forth the jump, added the spark of the cradle, the earth Angel, and then recited the first Kee as the knight was encased in the cylindrical energy of the jump.

The Timekeeper added, "Then through his charge and honourable duty, in which his love shall support the Empress, she will learn the lessons."

"It is as you say."

"As part of their acclimatisation, the language of the Malsimily shall arise within their awareness, and we have used realm-appropriate terms to describe her in ways different to other earthly women."

"Also, the knights must attract, invite, and progress the Empress's emotional, sensual, and physical senses sensitively. Romantic desires shall intensify as she becomes more evolved as well. Their spiritual connection, which shall be immediate, may at first remain somewhat hidden as it presents on a deeper level of their awareness."

"An instinctual, intuitive one." Clarified the Timekeeper, glancing at the Elevated One as their fingers worked.

"Indeed. Once this connection occurs, not only shall the knight be eloquent in using uniquely special phrases and words of the Malsimily during their most intimate moments ..."

"Words and phrases we shall include in their purest expression as we translate the words and thoughts of all who are entangled in the lives of the Empresses and the knights. As well as in one or two other areas of her story."

"It is as you say," agreed the Elevated One, "this shall add to their unwavering, undeniable sense of a deeply sacred, spiritual love."

At the approach of the second split, the Elevated One placed the second knight's seed within the circle of the earth. He shimmered up into human form, and his telepathic charge was given. Calling forth the jump, as the knight was encased in the jump cylinder, the Elevated One sent the spark of the cradle, the earth Angel, and then recited the second Kee.

"They all (*True Malsimily. Translation unavailable*). Therefore, their unique twin soul energy, which is of the Realm of the Empress, shall arise when they meet."

"They will fall deeply in love with one another, unify their energies and be as one," concluded the Timekeeper. The second knight was sent through, along with the Kee. The Elevated One then brought forth the third knight's seed. He shimmered up into human form, and his telepathic charge was given. As the third knight was encased in the jump's cylindrical energy, the Elevated One sent the spark of the cradle through; the earth Angel, then somewhat solemnly, recited the third Kee.

"She shall be drawn to the charmed books Spiritual Illumination, The Serenity Experience and (TM. TW). In the triple-layered way of the Malsimily, they become an initiating force, a trigger, and a seal for the incarnations and the knights. If read in order, the books provide a more evolved, in-depth version of the author's creative non-fiction memoir as was written under the previous title. The progressive state of the books is quite clear because although there were no interactive elements in Spiritual Illumination, The Serenity Experience included a few, with significantly more in (TM. TW)."

The third knight was sent through. The Elevated One brought forth the fourth seed and placed it within the circle of earth. He shimmered up into human form, and was given his telepathic charge. As he became encased in the energy of the jump, the Elevated One sent the earth Angel and the spark of the cradle through. Just before they recited the final Kee, the Timekeeper interrupted,

"We trust the books will indeed be helpful to her, for we have seen her enemies, and only the knights can help her defeat them. The Red Oracle, the Italian Mafia and the Watchers are tame compared to the most threatening of all, the Great Suffering. This deadly disease must not tarnish their ethereal value in any form, whether through another person or through a medical administering of the vaccine, prior to making the jump."

The Elevated One's face was tight with concentration. "It is, as you say, Timekeeper. We are aware of the risks. The virus must not be carried through to the other realms through her incarnations or the knights."

"A unified agreement," the Timekeeper said satisfactorily.

"Indeed. Then, providing the Empress makes it through all of that, she will have the Stone Harvest to stay when she returns."

"Can the Empress achieve these goals? Did we enlighten her enough?" Asked the Timekeeper, even though they knew how things would eventually pan out.

"We choose to think so. We must all do the best we can with what we have."

The Timekeeper agreed. "She shall know her purpose to unify the mind, body, and spirit trinity as her incarnated lives progress then?"

"That she will. Her mind – instinctive powers, shall give her a strong, unwavering purpose in the Land of Ludonia. In this mental subconscious realm, she shall learn of the Great Suffering, which shall be a critical factor in evolving her lesson on *Trauma*. Her spirit–intuitive powers shall ensure a strong core of spiritual integrity, which she shall master as the spiritual wife. In this incarnation, she shall evolve her *Transformation* fully so she may return to us and work towards becoming triumphant. Her body – sensitive powers, hmm, yes. She will feel an affinity with all that supports life and recognise the deeper cycles in play.

Yes, yes. As a dancer, for the initial unfoldment, she shall learn to ground her spiritual energies into the body and learn to trust her intuition. This journey shall lead her to the addressment point. Her interactions in the earthy judicial system called the Police, where she lives her spiritual truth fully through action, shall bring her closer to completing the physical aspect teachings of *Trust* and *Truth*."

"The knights shall protect her throughout, for it is their honourable charge to do so." Observed the Timekeeper. "They will risk their lives for her if need be."

"It is so." The Elevated One replied as they turned back to the knight in stasis and began to recite the fourth Kee. Once all four knights were sent through the jump, with the relevant Malsimily elements attached, the Elevated One sighed with relief. The Timekeeper began to turn away.

"We must prepare for their return at the jump gateway then."

The Elevated One turned their calm, benevolent smile upon the Timekeeper. "Wait a moment. As the situation is already upon us, and in case we do not get the opportunity later, may we observe a little of Empress Salliniquai's experience of love?" The crinkling around their eyes showed the Elevated One to be smiling indulgently.

"Of course. This is permitted." A brief tuck to one corner of their mouth was the only indication that the request amused the Timekeeeper.

Afterwards, the Elevated One observed, "Though the incarnation's lives were lonely to some degree, they must have been fairly interesting ones, too."

The Timekeeper cocked an eyebrow, which was quite out of character, and was quick to exclaim,

"More than interesting. Quite romantic, funny, and intriguing. We found ourselves gripped by the (*True Malsimily. Translation unavailable*), and we agree, it is indeed, as you say. Salliniquai should experience the greatest kind of love while she can, considering the weight of her charge and her responsibility when she returns. Yes. A fitting reward for all she will eventually face," The Timekeeper cleared their throat, floated closer and observed quietly. "You were a trifle hard on the Awakener, O Elevated One."

The Elevated One caught the Timekeeper's eye. "We know, we know. It was behaviour not in the vibration of the realm, we know."

"Ahh, well. All will be well in the end," the Timekeeper said enigmatically.

The Elevated One paused to glance at them. "You know this for sure?" All will be well in the end. But which end? They may be speaking of the end of her reign rather than the current situation. The Timekeeper stayed silent, unwilling to deny or confirm. Unable to, in fact. Bound by magic never to speak of events not yet come to pass, they usually inferred with statements that could be taken either way. "However, what is done is done. We can only move forward on the path laid before us." The Elevated One inclined their head a little. The sound of the approaching Stone Harvest seemed more intense. "We must hurry ..." They turned back to the altar.

"We have made it so the chance of their life paths crossing in the human physical realm is strong. Our thoughts were that this would be beneficial. What do you think?"

Used to the way the Timekeeper spoke with hints, rhetorical questions, and innuendos towards the outcome of events, they replied, "It is a positive possibility, yes, as they will be drawn to the same interests spiritually. Yes, their paths may cross. We, too, believe this to be a good thing."

The Timekeeper hovered forward, closer to the Elevated One. "What might happen if they meet?" they pressed.

"They will experience a strong sense of knowing one another, like deja vu. They will instinctively seek a friendship with one another."

"So, they will recognise their similar qualities and seek to retain the Brotherhood bond." The Timekeeper nodded, satisfied. "That is good. The Salliniquai incarnations shall be well protected then. We have wondered whether the knights might recognise the similarity for what it is, or might they think it simply a mad coincidence their women are all named after Salliniquai?"

There wass that strange reference again. "My dear Timekeeper, wonder away. Only you seem to have time to do so. Sometimes, we wish we could access the time streams as you do. If evolved enough, they may put it down to simply sharing a past life," suggested the Elevated One thoughtfully. "As we understand it, you narrowed the confines of the Empress's descent to one particular country."

"England, yes."

"And with your help, we sent the knights directly to Rowanshire. If we're lucky, the Empresses may be born in this created place; if not, they shall be naturally drawn there or brought there by the knights." The Elevated One seemed a bit happier with how the situation was turning out. As to the island portal, this was a place both real and known to the human physical realm, we presume?"

"Indeed." The Timekeeper replied, floating closer to the altar the Elevated One was working from. "We thought of Samoa and one or two others, but in the end, we decided on the island of Saint Lucia."

"The knights must also be aligned to the human life years of the oldest knight. Born in the late sixties, he shall have up to fifty-five years to complete his charge. The other three shall be born after him, and if all goes as we hope, they will find, love, guide, and then return with their Salliniquai incarnations," said the Elevated One. Thoughtfully considering the years the knights would have upon the earth, the Timekeeper offered some interesting facts.

"They shall be born just in time to experience, by far, the best most lively and most colourful decade in earth's history, labelled as such for many reasons. Iconic aquarian artists included ..."

The Elevated One arched an interested eyebrow as they interrupted. "Oh? Such as?"

"Well, let's see—the good things like Motown and Disco ..." they paused, and their eyes began to glow. "They will grow up in the decade when one of the greatest Nubian musical geniuses of all time was influencing British people with reggae music. He made a massive impact on the world by infusing the Nubian people with a sense of themselves, truth, hope, and love. He spread the message of one love to the world. One of the greatest Aquarian water-bearers of all time, the Legendary Bob Marley. His passing was one of the greatest losses for the coming of the Aquarian age, and The Third Way ..." Caught up in the moment, the Timekeeper sighed. "The documentary, When Bob Marley Came to Britain, will not be made until August 2020, unfortunately, but we hope that through watching it, the people of the earth may appreciate how he was open to building bridges, unity, the Third Way, and will try to remember and carry his message of love in their hearts." Recovering marginally, they added, "David Bowie was another famous Aquarian. Like no other, he stood out in his original music and style of genius. Not quite our cup of tea, but hey, such is life. In terms of making an impact and garnering the attention of millions through their political views and actions for peace, equality, and safety for their people, Mahatma Gandhi, and Nelson Mandela." In a musing tone, they continued. "Back then there was also Abba, Otis Redding, Earth, Wind and Fire, and Donna Summer. Movies like Enter the Dragon, Planet of the Apes, and The Warriors. TV shows like Wonder Woman, The Incredible Hulk, Randall and Hopkirk - deceased, Mission Impossible, Star Trek, Children of the Stones, and Dr. Who, among many others." To the Elevated One's surprise, the Timekeeper's face was almost glowing in its animation as they recalled the strange details. "Then there were Chopper bikes, roller skates and roller discos: Walkman's, platform shoes, and flared trousers. Yes, hippie chic and glamour were quite fabulous then. It underpins feminine fashion and free expression in a bohemian style to this day. Oh, and of course, peasant blouses, maxi dresses, and others with an ethnic theme..."

The Elevated One was staring at them, stunned. They had never heard the Timekeeper speak with this much passion before. The depth of the human emotional energy transferred whilst experiencing or, more accurately, while witnessing the Empress's lives on the earth had affected their sensibilities.

Having caught the perplexed, scrutinising gaze of the Elevated One, the Timekeeper decided to discontinue their explanation. They could have given a longer, more interesting list, but they knew the Elevated One would comprehend only a little of it. Their features relaxed back into their usual neutral expression as they changed the subject.

"The protection of Salliniquai's true identity in the game of Snakes and Ladders was dealt with. It was left to the clown to guide her."

"Then the High Malsimily thought dispersal spell worked on the clown and the brothers Saxon and Noxas?"

"It was never sent. As we understand it, as the situation was a trial, it did not involve a mature Salliniquai Incarnation. It did not have the objective of teaching one of the four lessons. As to the rest of it, working through young Sally, Salliniquai now has a direct way of wielding great grace worldwide, strengthening its spiritual integrity. She must also be protected."

"This was how we understood it, too. We used a specific incident to get her to the island, which ensured her safety before the Great Suffering could affect her."

"A specific incident?"

"Literally, yes. A family situation drew her to the island. But you know all this Timekeeper. It must be frustrating not to be able to speak of such events, or maybe not, according to your unique way of existence."

"What about the Empress Sallee with the youngest of the brothers, Benton, in the Land of Ludonia? How can we ensure they return when they are required to?"

After a moment more of staring at the Timekeeper, who stared back expressionless, the Elevated One responded.

"Again, it is different due to how time works in Ludonia. As they return through the jump, the knight's years in Ludonia should not change his true age from twenty-four. Or should we say, *if* they return through the jump? Are we correct in our assessment of these circumstances, Timekeeper?"

A long moment passed. Unable to reveal any details involving timelines, the Timekeeper replied.

"We shall await them all at Jump gateway." Their words confirmed the Elevated One's hope of Empress Salliniquai and the four knights returning as expected. By not answering directly, saying instead that they were going to the Jump gateway to await them all, they answered our question without answering the question. If the assessment had been incorrect, they would have responded quite differently. The Elevated One spoke of how they had ensured matters would progress as they directed.

"Having cast one of my most complicated spells, the incarnations shall speak the triggers to awaken the knights at the appointed time. The awakening trigger cannot be activated by accident and only within two days of the jump date."

"An excellacious, most valuable consideration. How did you make sure of that?"

The Elevated One explained that to ensure the chosen hosts would not be harmed by the potent energy of the Empresserial orb, which had to be drawn down and infused with the

Empresserial trigger, they charmed their own earth Angel—an author whose writing inspired them and allowed the energy to divide into the three books mentioned earlier.

"Only the Dream Knight, young Sally, and the Empress Salliniquai's incarnations will be aware of the True Malsimily nature of the books.

"We understand the purpose of this."

"Young Sally's exposure is shielded until she comes of age, however. The adult Incarnations shall be naturally drawn to these books as ultimately (*True Malsimily. Translation unavailable*) eyes. As long as they have laid their hands upon it and read it themselves, the Empresserial energy shall continue to reveal its nature to them."

The Timekeeper was nodding agreeably. "Understood. We gather these same three books are special enough to do much to awaken humans to the oldest and wisest aspects of spiritual knowledge as well?"

"That is so. We charged the author to create the series to trigger Salliniquai's Empresserial energy in all five of her earthly forms. However, we could only use the skills of A. T. Flowers on three occasions to ensure they remained potent." The Elevated One explained. *(T02).*

"Excellacious. And regardless of the span of earthly years the events took place in, the evolution of the empresserial energy presents to us in the order of her lessons. That is part of how we know when the time of her return approaches. Therefore, it is also the way of my translations. Can the humans discern the magical elements within the books?"

"We believe not, no. Although, if open to the truth of the nature of Divine spirituality, then yes, it may be so to some small degree.

"A suitable, unequivocally astute plan, Elevated One." The Timekeeper replied in a complementary tone. "How is the Dream

185

knight doing in his search for the Emperor's Books of Stone, which have infiltrated the human physical realm?"

"You know the answer to that better than we do. As the Empress's energy is divided into four, each incarnation shall connect with one of the Books of Stone, which shall materialise in her presence. Very helpful to the Dream Knights charge. However, as the Dream Knight cannot cross over to the realm of Ludonia, the Sallee incarnation must destroy the Wrong King's Book of Stone herself.

Just as we have ensured our three charmed books have the power to call to the Empress, refresh her energy and be a valuable aid in her spiritual development, however, the emperor's books had powers too. The Book of Stone, in its single form, has an energy thrice as potent as our three books, and as you know, it has the power to corrupt the minds of the masculine. One has found its way into the Land of Ludonia, which is why one of the Empresses will be summoned there to neutralise it. The Empresses shall recognise its destructive power and deal with it in the only way they can without their Empresserial powers, with the assistance of the Dream Knight, who shall continue to carry out his two-fold charge of releasing the spirits of humans from evil and destroying the Books of Stone.

Of the nine copies brought into the world, the four touched by the mature Empresses shall lose their power when she reads from them. When the three in the human physical realm touch the Book of Stone the Dream Knight appears astrally projected and their astral selves can communicate. Fortunately, not all who become one with the Dream Knight are evil. For much of the time, they travel harmlessly through the feminine and gain support from certain types, such as those who have transitioned. These people, once touched, are left with a strong sense of clarity around their identity, a boost to their confidence, and a strong desire for equality."

"The Dream Knight's passage through time shall be translated by us. Fortunately, our magically created county of Rowanshire is protected from the Books of Stone. None are within the boundary."

"Do you know how many the Dream Knight has yet to find?"

"As he has destroyed the books empowered by the Cold King and the Abusive King, there are two remaining."

"We trust he will be successful in his charge."

"As do we. We were curious about something Elevated One. Why did you set the third book for publication after the year 2024? The Empress and her knights will have returned to the realm long before then. What use will it be to them?"

"No use to them, but valuable for humans. Especially following the worst effects of the Great Suffering. Along with Pluto being in Aquarius for the next two decades, it will be one of the many important treasures helping to steer the people towards the path of ... well, you know the details of all of this; we need not go over it. Now, work with us to seal all we have done to support the Empresses and the knights." The Timekeeper did so, and after a few moments, they let go of the staff both had been holding.

"Thank you for your assistance, Timekeeper."

"At your summoning, we shall return."

"For now, you may travel."

Seemingly reluctant to go, the Timekeeper said. "Remember, we are but a shimmer away. Bid thy return, and we will do so," they offered, strangely poignant.

"As you say. Now, we must transfer the remaining essences to the staff."

"Of course." The Timekeeper clasped their hands together. "For the love of Empress Salliniquai."

"For the love of Empress Salliniquai." The Elevated One returned.

The two bowed benevolently towards one another, and then the Timekeeper backed away, drawing their hood back over their head. They turned and shimmered away, knowing they would never see the Elevated One in this form again.

Once the Timekeeper departed, the Elevated One's gaze fixed upon the wide opening of their geode. A dark grey sludge had crossed the boundary and was slowly spreading towards them. They shook their head in despair.

So soon...? Working quickly but calmly, they continued weaving the spell required to supercharge the Empress's energy at the time of the Offering into the staff. At each pause in the mantra, voiced in High Malsimily, the staff sent out an answering glow, with the scent of Raynorlorium filling the air each time, giving the sense that, on some subtle level, a conversation was taking place.

Once the staff was charmed, they paused to consider the situation brought forth by the irresponsible actions of the Empress, wondering whether they had failed in their duty to evolve her nature to a reasonable level. She was due to learn specific life lessons with them when she slipped away, they thought regretfully—then reconsidered. No. They had not failed the Empress. With the swift actions of all concerned, they managed to salvage the situation satisfactorily.

They gasped suddenly. The Stone Harvest was three feet from the dais they stood upon. From their position in front of the large stone altar, topped with strangely shaped containers holding powders, liquids (*True Malsimily, translation unavailable*), elements, bubbles, and hair, among other things, which can only be described in Malsimily, the Elevated One murmured an incantation and the altar shimmered into the unseen. As they turned to look behind them again, they found themselves stuck. Looking down, they saw that the Stone Harvest had crept right beneath their feet in those few seconds, trapping them where they stood.

By the Empress, no! Their thoughts returned to the Empress. She had not learned the final lesson! She may not realise the key to safely entering the Distance is (*True Malsimily. Translation unavailable*). The Timekeeper cannot disclose this information to her due to their discretionary rule of binding. Could it be we have failed in our charge? No, it cannot be so. It is not in the spirit of the realm to think in such a way. We must not underestimate the Empress! By the time she reaches the Distance, she will have matured enough to figure it out. With the earth Angels and the knight's support, she should be able to hold her own on the human physical realm, even without her Empresserial powers. As soon as she returns, we shall communicate our situation.

***

The Awakener, meanwhile, had arrived at the enormous, cavernous structure known as the Cradle, sitting within its own magically enhanced field, after orbing through the travel wells. They advised the Alchemist of the current situation, enjoying the ever-present, potent aroma of Raynorlorium as they did so. For those not of the Malsimily, this is translated as lemons, which do not exist in the Realm of the Empress. In this realm, it is a scent arising naturally from the realm waters due to the trail of energy the seed fairies travelling through it leave behind.

The Cradle's welcoming, abundantly healthy, lush-green

appearance was a little deceptive, for it was also a place of protection that could magically defend itself if needed. Inside, it had a misty, moist interior, with the sound of rushing water continually present due to the vast, dominating waterfall.

Thoughtfully considering the information shared by the Awakener, the Alchemist smiled brightly and said,

"The Empress requires the crown for the Offering at the Distance, of course," as they gently stroked the long curl protruding from the left side of their close-cropped, golden-black hair. As they walked sedately down the broad steps that formed a narrow, inwardly spiralling staircase within the crater of the crown, their layered robe of a soft pink hue billowed out around them. With an enigmatic smile that lit up their dark brown face, the sentimental, softly spoken Alchemist focused on the task at hand.

When the Alchemist reached the deepest part of the crater, they sprinkled a magical powder over the crown, which sent a low hum around the space, tipped out the liquid from a small container retrieved from the sleeve of their robe, and with a swirl of their hands created a cloud of blue-hued smoke, which wafted around them in a spiralling fashion as they spoke in Malsimily. Once the construction of the spell was complete; they turned and began walking back up the spiral stairs. After a few moments, seven misty layers of colour, a chakra rainbow with the base colour at the bottom, began to appear. Solidifying into a formation of wide bands of colour, they created a funnel for the crown to rise through.

"The crown must pass through all seven chakras before we can remove it." The Alchemist explained, fingering their precious, palm-sized amulet of the symbol of Venus, hanging just below their solar plexus on the outside of their robe.

"Is it a long process?" The Awakener wondered, leaning forward to look down into the crater. They held back the two waist-long, silver-black braids hanging forwards over their shoulders, which took on the appearance of liquid when out in the sunlight, as they did so.

"It is a beautiful one."

"It is as you say." Replied the Awakener, moving to stand beside the Alchemist. Both looked down into the crater for a few minutes, studying the shifting mists and thickening colours. As the Awakener told them more of what had taken place at the geodes, the Alchemist strolled around the crater, studying the progress of the materialising crown.

"Fortunately, the Empress was too young to use the Jump and was flower-petalled instead. An opportunity to slow the time stream so we could send the knights after her was a blessing we are sure the Elevated One appreciated," the Alchemist said after mulling over the Awakener's accounting of the events. As the youngest of the four androgynous beings, the Awakener was not necessarily as fully aware of the broader intricacies of evolving the Empress or the details of her time spent with the other three beings. Their gaze lowered, and their expression grew uncertain, hinting at their doubt. Astutely, the Alchemist observed.

"You remain concerned for the Empress, Awakener. For her lessons with the knights?"

"And for her safe return, yes, we do. We are responsible for this divisional thing happening."

"Do not fret so." The Alchemist said kindly. "The situation is already in play; we are all working together, and the knights were brought forth and charged to fulfil the first part of their purpose on earth." Their head tilted slightly, and as the only one of the four androgynous beings able to make physical contact with the others, they touched the Awakener again.

"It is not in the spirit of the realm to dwell on what is perceived as regretful actions. Living on the earth was within the scope of their markers. Otherwise, that course of rectification would not have been available to the Elevated One." Their kind, meaningful gaze was reassuring.

The tension in the Awakener's features smoothed out a bit.

"It is, of course, as you say. It is just, with the fate of all three realms bound to the success of the Empress fulfilling her purpose, we thought ..."

The Alchemist held up a hand and smiled indulgently.

"We have every faith the Empress can hold her own on such a difficult, corrupt world." They both turned to look down into the crater again. The crown had formed more solidly into the seen and had begun its ascent. The Alchemist continued. "This is where the age of Aquarius shall succeed in saving countless hearts and souls."

"As we understand it, the emperor has (*True Malsimily. Translation unavailable*), with his Books of Stone."

"Yes, unfortunately." The Alchemist's huge, snow-white karm, padded past them, lavender eyes glinting mysteriously. It crossed behind the waterfall, and entered one of the chambers beyond.

Remembering the Timekeeper's strange references, the Awakener said.

"We would like to learn more about the earth. It has become intriguing to us. The Empress might explain the new things added to her knowledge during her lives."

"Perhaps, if enough memories remain with her. Did you not ask the Elevated One about this? You might have been given a vision through the Timekeeper's grasp of the staff or, in fact, from the Timekeeper themselves, just as we did."

The Awakener pulled a pinched, sheepish expression that looked out of place on their long, light-skinned face, contrasting starkly with their waist-long, silver-black hair. "We didn't like to ask. The Elevated One was quite busy rectifying our ..." They paused, a self-conscious tone to their voice. "They were beginning to lose patience with us for ... for ..."

"They realise it was through no fault of your own," the Alchemist said kindly, again lightly resting a hand on the Awakener's arm.

"We trust it to be so," they murmured. "Your nurturing words bring hope and relief, Alchemist."

"As is our duty." They turned to look down into the crater again. The crown had risen above the base chakra band of colour. After observing the rising crown, the Alchemist advised, "When she arrives back as the four incarnations, the unifying ritual will need to proceed with all speed before the kurren-see can be exchanged."

"Indeed. We understand the urgent importance of this." The Awakener was silent momentarily, considering another question they wished to ask. "The Timekeeper once said it can take as many as thirty earth years from the actual moment of transfer for the influence of the Pisces age to no longer have a hold over humankind."

"Indeed, this is so. Without the conditioning of religion, politics, economics, science, and capitalism interrupting the progression of the Aquarian age."

The Awakener required clarification. "But then, how does humankind evolve?"

"Through the Third Way, which will remain unseen until the balance tips in favour of spirituality. Unfortunately, the influence of Uranus on the Aquarian age is a double-edged sword. With AI software, algorithms, flash fiction, and tik-tok mentalities, earthly attention spans are short, patience practically non-existent, inspirational creativity seems to be a thing of the past, and encouraging a deeper understanding of the qualities of life that support longevity has fallen by the wayside in favour of short-term pleasures.

The life experience, qualifications, knowledge, and sound advice from those past their mid-life point no longer seem of value or interest to most of the younger generations. To some degree, this is entirely understandable since the older generation is being blamed for bringing the world to the edge of its destruction. Only by embracing the Third Way mentality can things progress in a way which brings global support, compassion, and trust among people."

The Awakener was stunned by the overwhelming, uphill struggle those wishing to progress spiritual change faced and, again, noticed the strange earthly references. "It seems a complicated process ..."

"Only to those residing on the Earth. Not to those aware of the whole picture."

"We are expressly relieved by your words," said the Awakener.

"All shall arrive at jump gateway shortly. Make haste, while we ready ourselves for the part we must play."

"As you say, Alchemist. The Empress will expect our presence on her arrival. We will not fail her again. For the love of the Empress."

The Alchemist turned for a moment, bowing slightly towards the Awakener. "For the love of the Empress."

STELLA FLETTON

Epilogue

In the human physical realm, known as the planet Earth...

When the unseen moon was new and the night was at its darkest, eight fabulously bright stars from the Realm of the Empress raced across the vast expanse, lighting up the sky. These were not your average, run-of-the-mill shooting stars, however, for these carried the essence of Empress Salliniquai and her four good knights of the Brotherhood of the Nine.

As transcendent time travellers, they pierced their way through Earth's history with a unique purpose to join with newly born and young humans of a particular energy. Chosen to host and progress the crucial aspects of Empress Salliniquai's nature and powers, once all the life experiences have been accomplished, the Empress and her knights are destined to return to the Realm of the Empress. A realm governed by the Malsimily but created by the Empress.

The end.

The Quest of Salliniquai

The Salliniquai Chronicles

The mighty Empress Salliniquai is from a spiritual realm and desires the experience of human love. After completing an earth-based trial, Salliniquai sneaks off on a second trip to Earth and causes a glitch during her transportation. She gets more than she bargained for when her spiritual nature is infused into four different women. Incarnations. Each incarnation must complete a lesson on human behaviour on Earth, aided by Knights of the Brotherhood of the Nine in their human forms, before the Empress can return to her realm.

The Trial of Salliniquai prequels the full-length adult novels that form *The Salliniquai Chronicles*. For your human interest, summaries are included below.

New Adult/Adult Fantasy Fiction

The Trial of Salliniquai. A small but mighty standalone, or a prequel to The Salliniquai Chronicles.

Adult Women's Fiction/Romantic Fantasy

The Trauma Host (in the Land of Ludonia). Book One.
In the first of Salliniquai's lives upon the earth, she incarnates as reluctant heroine Sallee Bhiru-shah, a virgin schoolteacher from the county of Rowanshire who takes a tumble down the stairs that leaves her in a coma. With her ambitious plans of teaching at a school in India or England ending abruptly, she is not too happy when she finds herself in the Land of Ludonia in her subconscious, charged to complete a quest. A magical fantasy adventure with romance and a few laughs thrown in.

The Trust Host. Book Two.
Winner of A Woman's Write Best Unpublished Novel, 2022.
In the second of Salliniquai's lives upon the earth, she incarnates as Hippie Chick Sallie Chambers, an underprivileged orphan turned professional dancer with a somewhat paranoid view of the world, a prickly phobia of men and trust issues, who is quite the fish out of water when she accepts a dancing job far from home aboard a glamourous Italian cruise ship. Things become complicated and spiral out of control during the World Cup 1990, when smuggling and murder turn her dream job into a disaster. A Women's Fiction/Romantic Fantasy novel with a touch of magic.

The Book of Malsimily Translations. Volume 1
Translations from The Trial of Salliniquai, The Trauma Host (in the Land of Ludonia), and The Trust Host.

The Truth Host. Book Three.
In the third of Salliniquai's lives upon the earth, she incarnates as scarred-faced Sallyanne Roserie. It is a fight all the way for bohemian Sallyanne for as a woman of conscience, she faces

discrimination, tough challenges, dubious intentions, and secret groups within the British police service, one of which is hell-bent on bringing her down. A Women's Fiction/Romantic Fantasy novel with a touch of magic.

The Transformation Host. Book Four.
In the fourth of Salliniquai's lives upon the earth, she incarnates as Sallori Tessler, a fed up, forty-year-old, disillusioned vicar's wife of eighteen years, who spontaneously throws caution to the wind following the death of her parents, discovering she was adopted, and losing her best friend, whom the entire local church of England congregation has labelled a devil worshipper. Giving up on her marriage and her Christian faith, she travels a new spiritual path with a motley crew of pagans allowing her bohemian nature to blossom. A Women's Fiction/Romantic Fantasy novel with high romance, a few good laughs, and a touch of magic.

The Triumphs of Salliniquai. Book Five.
In the Triumphs of Salliniquai, it is action all the way as the Empresses, four androgynous beings, and four Knights of the Brotherhood of the Nine return to the Realm of the Empress only to find it is a race against time to cross dangerous, magically infused, living fields to reach the place of the Offering before the Stone Harvest corrupts the land, and Salliniquai's onward journey through extraordinary realms of many wonders to challenge the emperor. A magical adventure.

The Book of Malsimily Translations. Volume 2
Translations from The Truth Host, The Transformation Host, and The Triumphs of Salliniquai (in the Realm of the Empress).

The Trial of Salliniquai

About the author

A spiritual warrior.

Aquarius Stella Fletton is an Indigo child on a Twin Flame journey. She lives a simple, quietly eccentric life with her family in Saint Lucia. As a Water-bearer, Stella recognizes that the transit of Pluto into Aquarius is timely to sharing her spiritual novels with all who believe in the benefits of the Aquarian age and desire a better, fairer future for all. As a champion of equality, Stella embraces diversity and supports the feminine in all her impressive aspects, by which she means women, nature, and the earth. Uplifting, inspirational, and fun, The Salliniquai Chronicles sparkle with positive, feminine strength.

What Stella wishes to achieve with her stories.
I hope the journey of Salliniquai illuminates readers in new and exciting ways whilst encouraging thoughts on how we may fix that which is not right in ourselves or in our world. These books highlight the best and the worst aspects of our society through a focus on real life, current events, issues of equality, and women's liberation.

Thanks for reading! I would love to know your thoughts. You can add a review of this novel on Amazon!

Printed in Great Britain
by Amazon

40665928R00121